DATE DUE

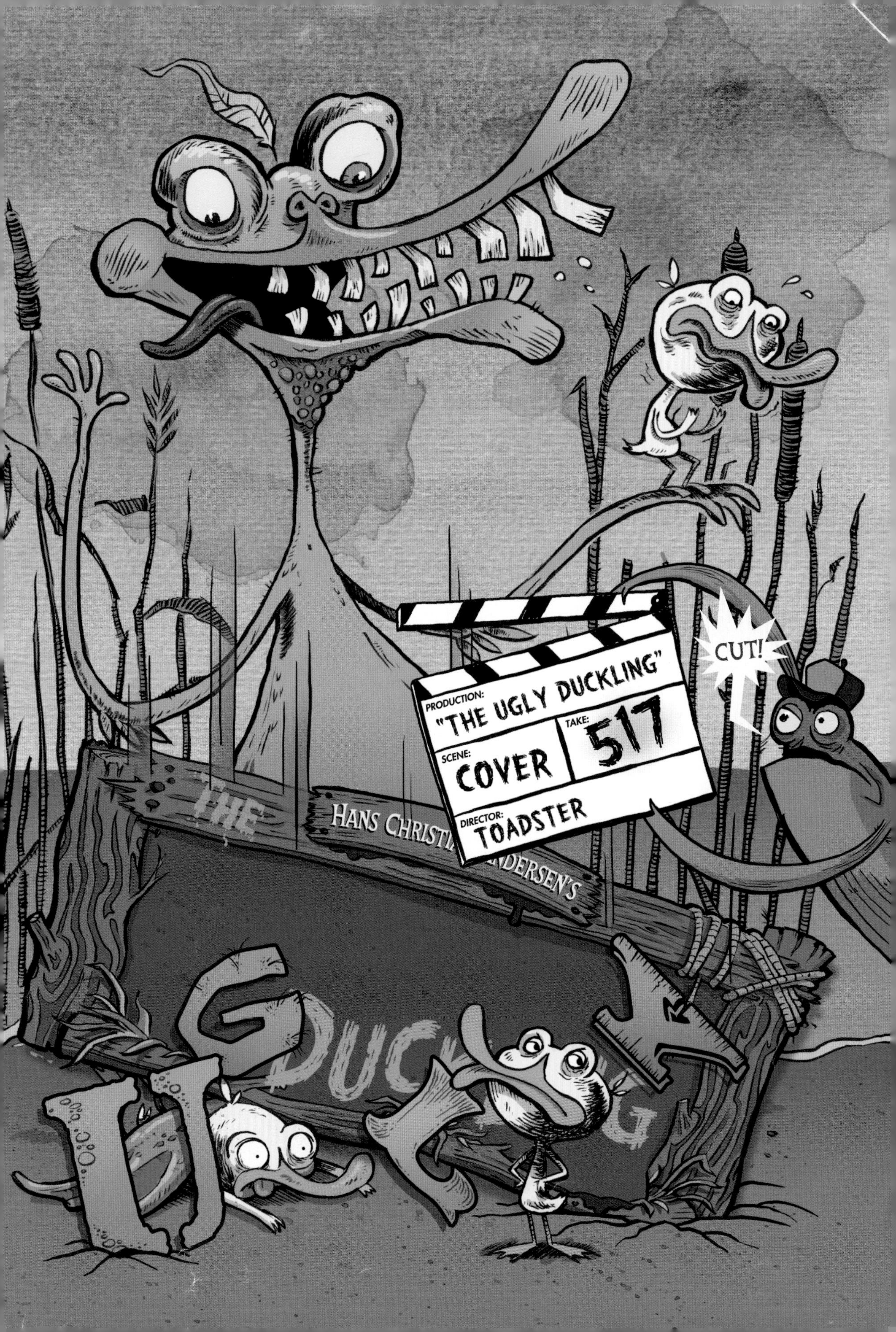
THE
HANS CHRISTIAN ANDERSEN'S
PRODUCTION:
"THE UGLY DUCKLING"
TAKE:
517
SCENE:
COVER
DIRECTOR:
TOADSTER
CUT!

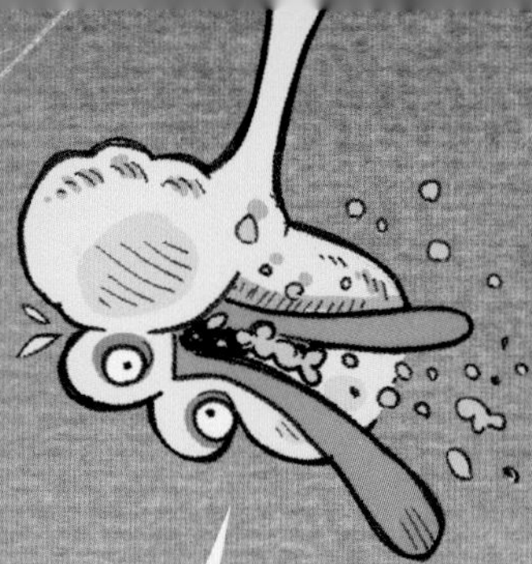

Graphic Spin is published by Stone Arch Books
151 Good Counsel Drive, P.O. Box 669
Mankato, Minnesota 56002
www.stonearchbooks.com

Library of Congress Cataloging-in-Publication Data

Powell, Martin.
The ugly duckling : the graphic novel / by Hans Christian Andersen ; retold by Martin Powell ; illustrated by Aaron Blecha.
p. cm. -- (Graphic spin)
ISBN 978-1-4342-1593-2 (library binding) -- ISBN 978-1-4342-1742-4 (pbk.)
1. Graphic novels. [1. Graphic novels. 2. Fairy tales.] I. Blecha, Aaron, ill. II. Andersen, H. C. (Hans Christian), 1805-1875. Grimme ælling. III. Title.
PZ7.7.P69Ug 2010
741.5'973--dc22

2009010530

Summary: Mother Duck waits for her last egg to hatch. When the odd little egg finally breaks open, Mother Duck is shocked to see an ugly duckling staring up at her. Despite its homeliness, Mother Duck adores her awkward child and does her best to protect him. Unfortunately, he is driven from the farm to fend for himself. Survival, however, takes more than good looks, and the plucky little duck plods bravely into the wilderness.

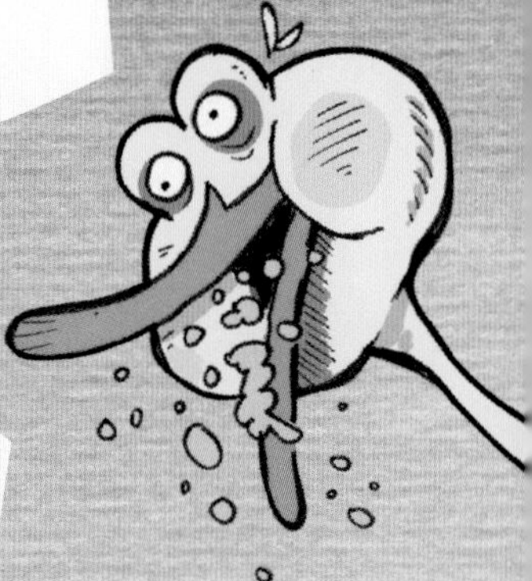

Designed by Bob Lentz
Edited by Donald Lemke
Directed by Heather Kindseth

Printed in the United States of America

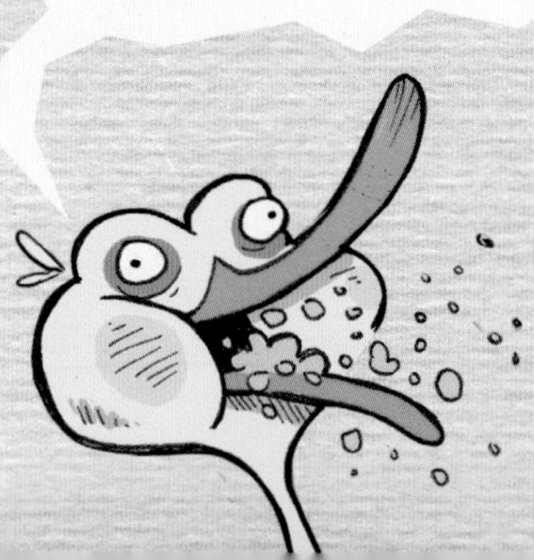

HANS CHRISTIAN ANDERSEN'S

THE UGLY DUCKLING

The Graphic Novel

retold by Martin Powell
illustrated by Aaron Blecha

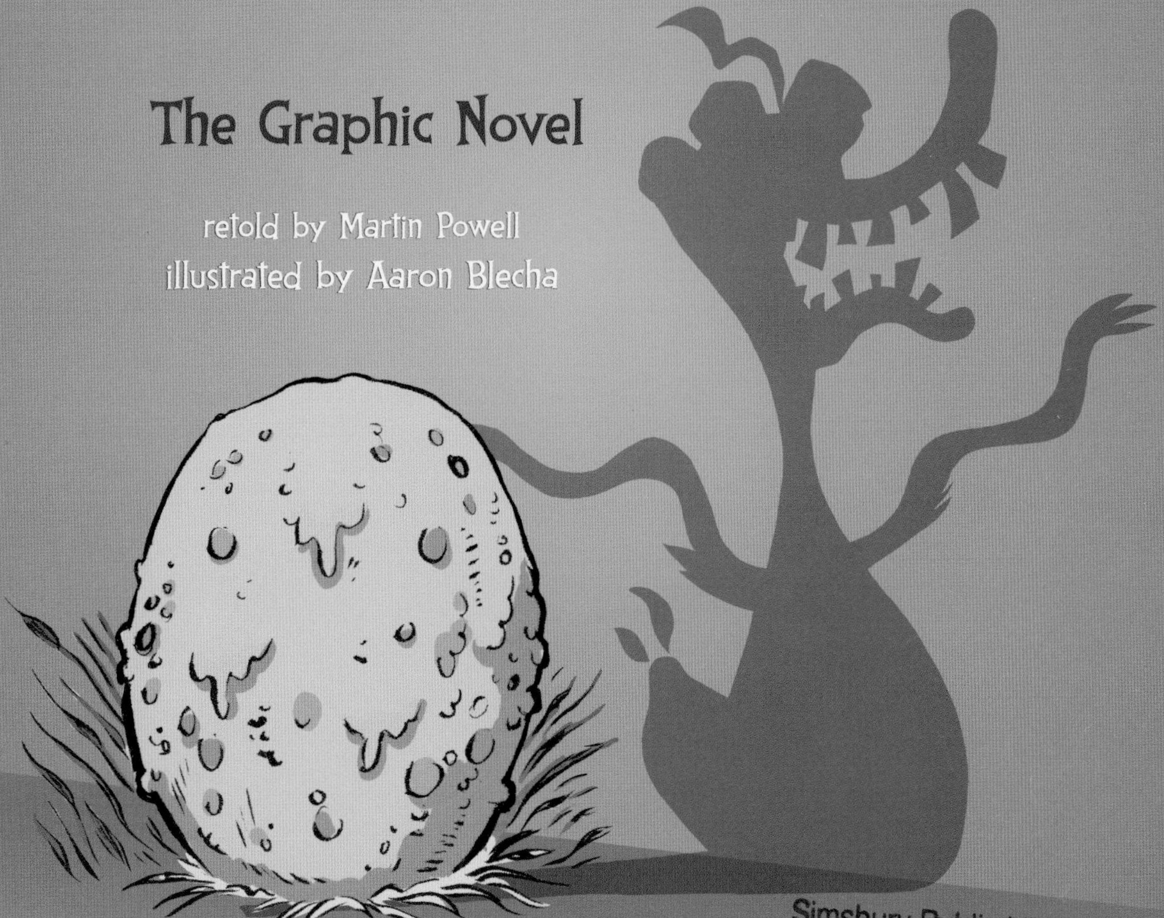

STONE ARCH BOOKS
MINNEAPOLIS SAN DIEGO

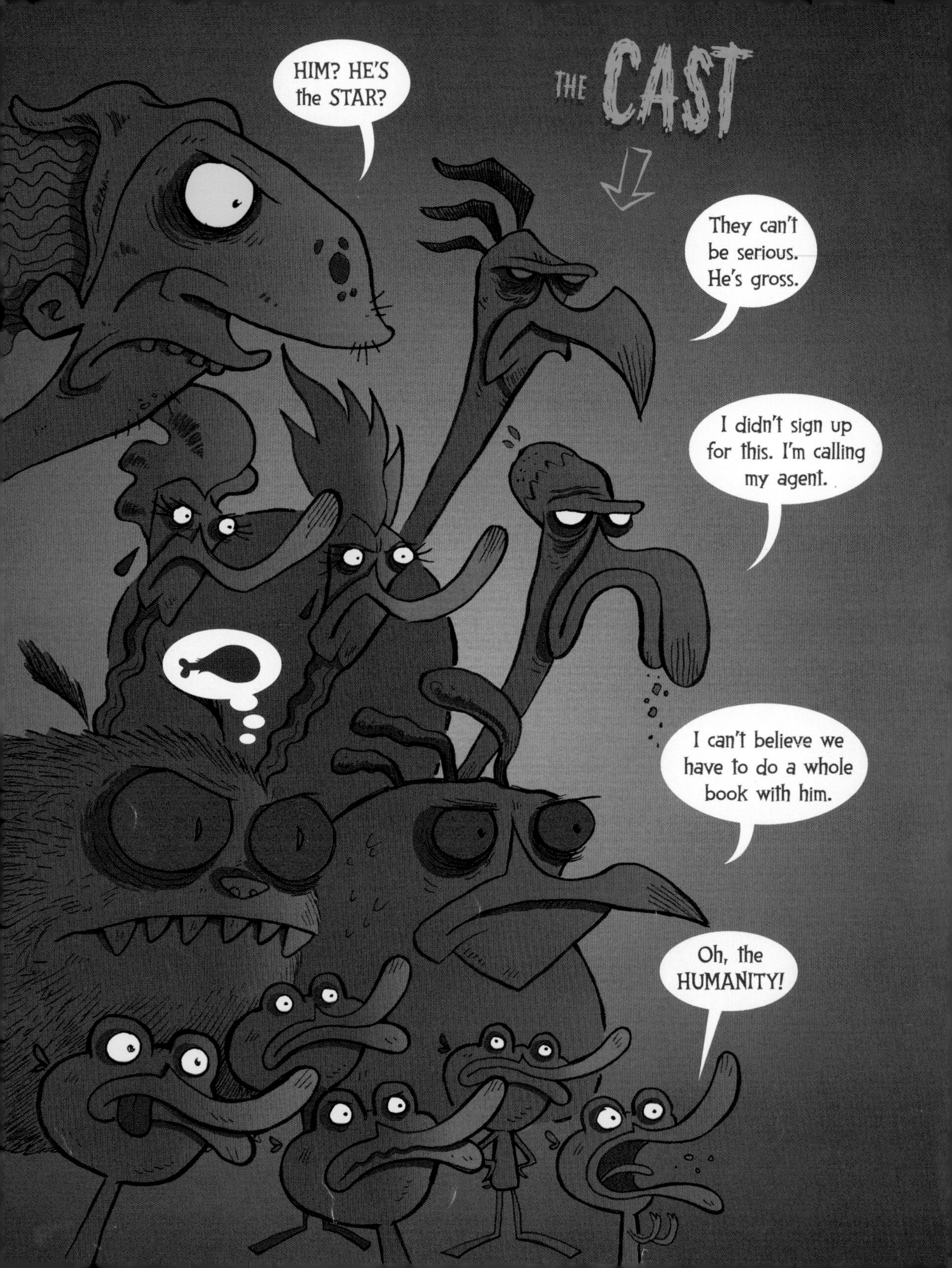
THE CAST
HIM? HE'S the STAR?
They can't be serious. He's gross.
I didn't sign up for this. I'm calling my agent.
I can't believe we have to do a whole book with him.
Oh, the HUMANITY!

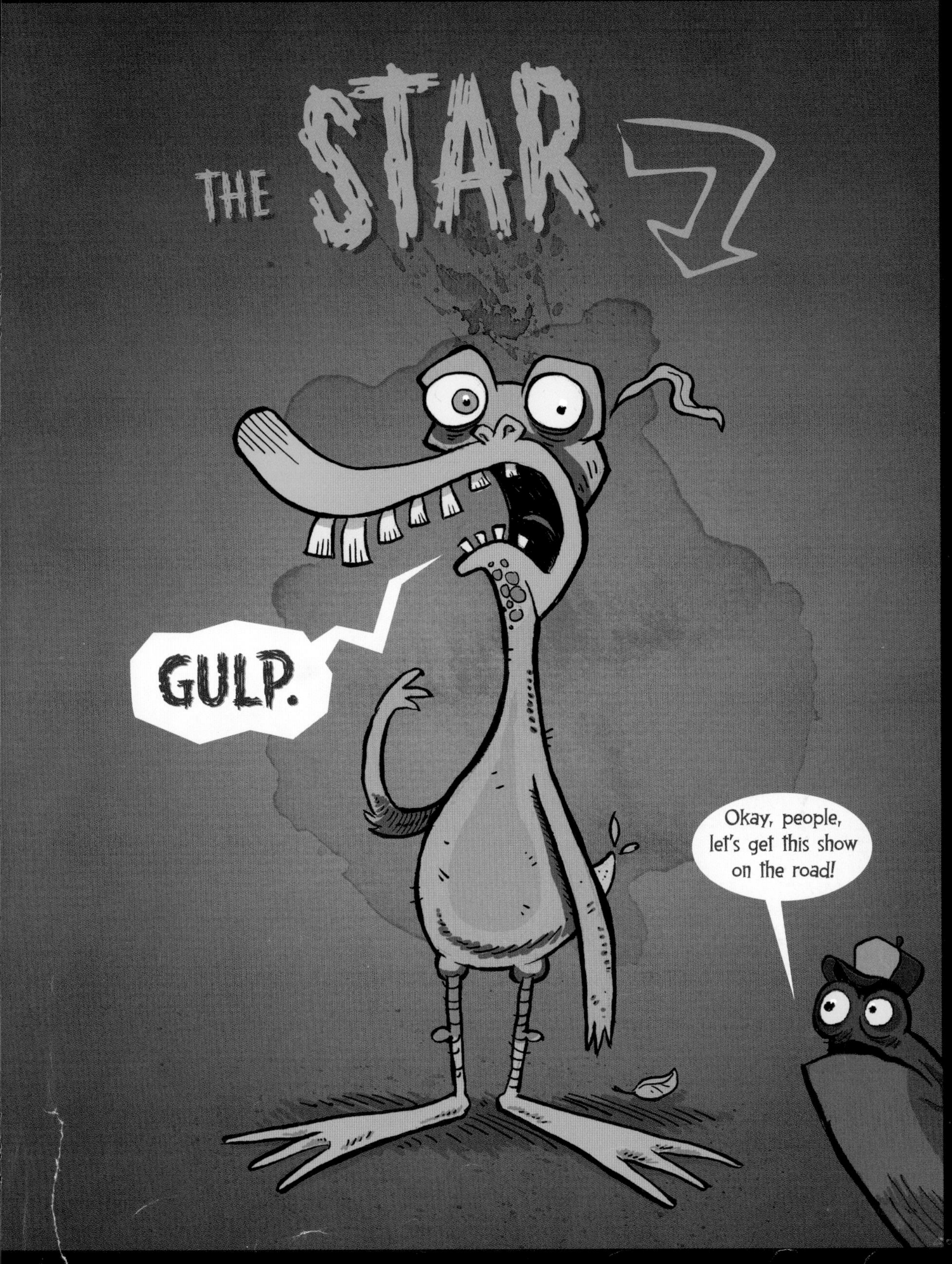
THE STAR
GULP.
Okay, people, let's get this show on the road!

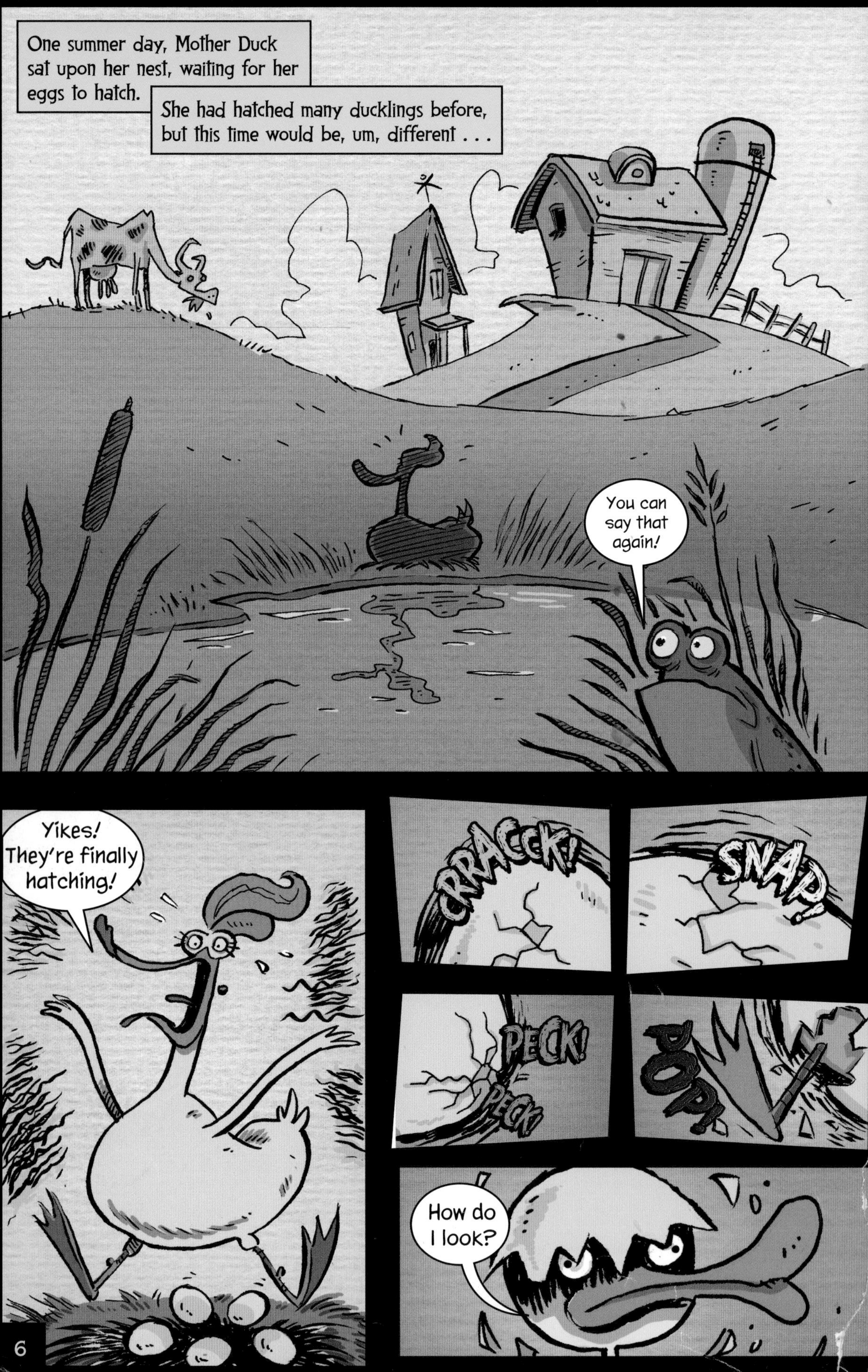
One summer day, Mother Duck sat upon her nest, waiting for her eggs to hatch.
She had hatched many ducklings before, but this time would be, um, different . . .
You can say that again!
Yikes! They're finally hatching!
CRACCK!
SNAP!
PECK!
PECK!
POP!
How do I look?

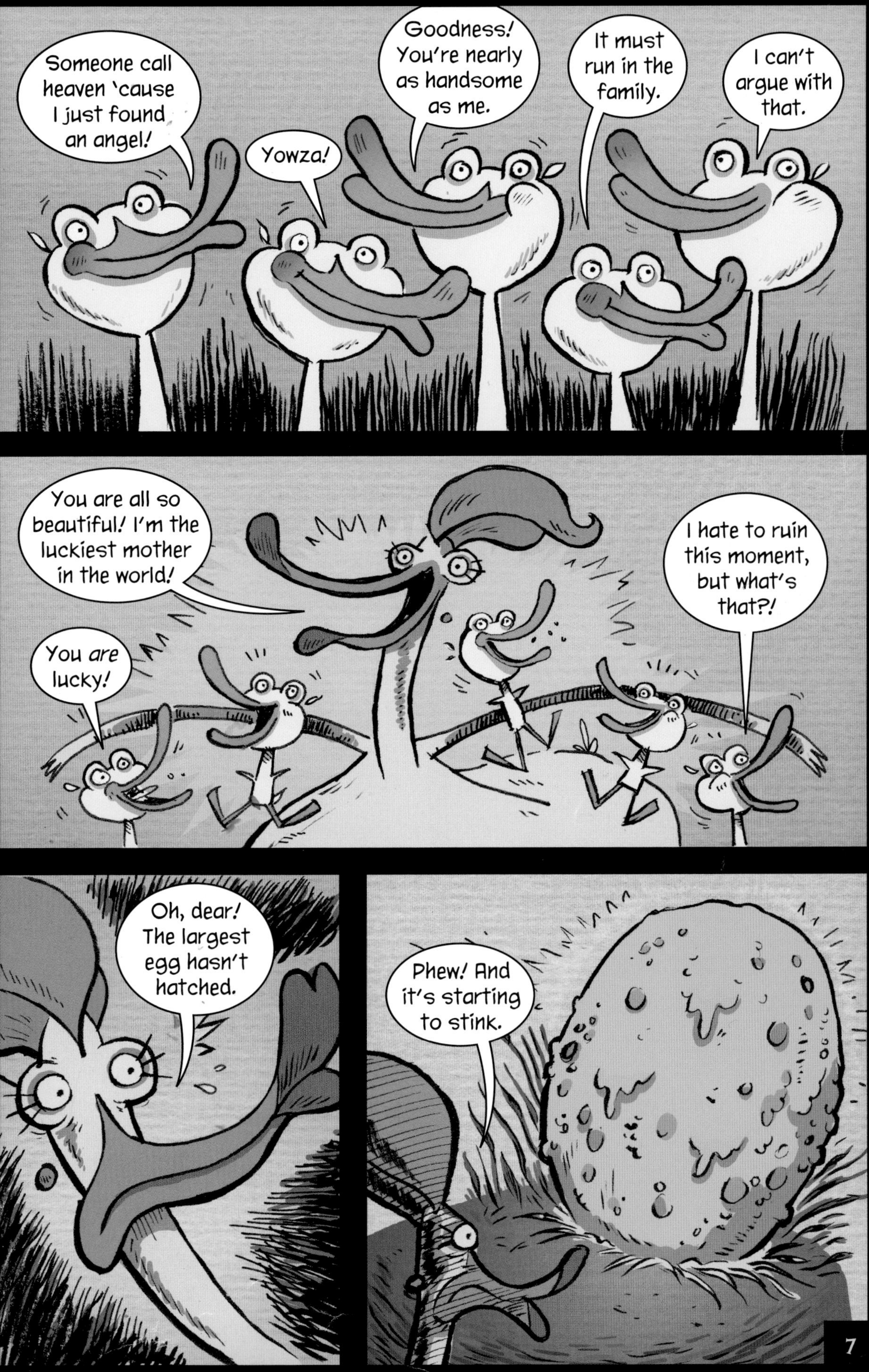
Someone call heaven 'cause I just found an angel!
Yowza!
Goodness! You're nearly as handsome as me.
It must run in the family.
I can't argue with that.
You are all so beautiful! I'm the luckiest mother in the world!
You are lucky!
I hate to ruin this moment, but what's that?!
Oh, dear! The largest egg hasn't hatched.
Phew! And it's starting to stink.

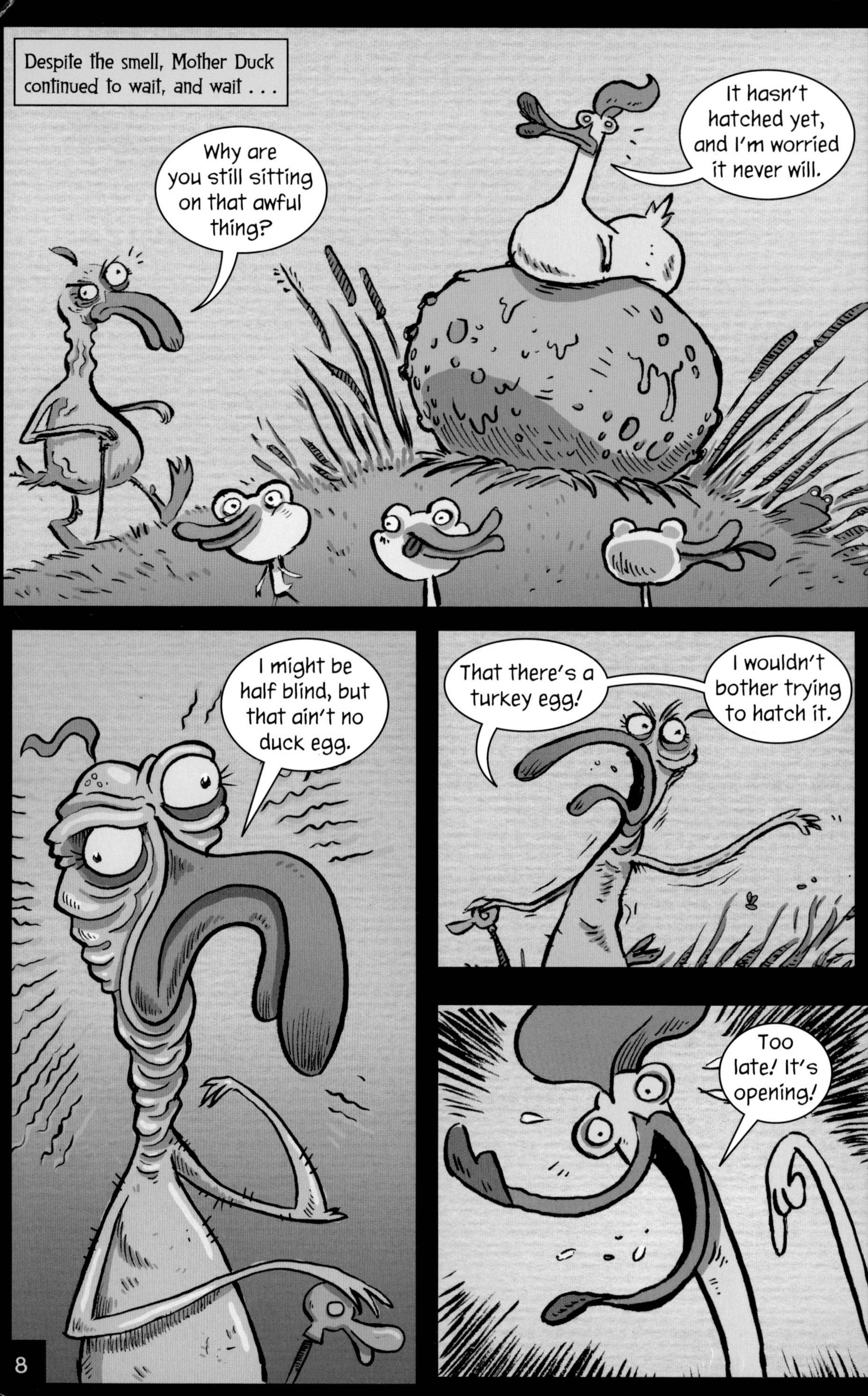
Despite the smell, Mother Duck continued to wait, and wait . . .
Why are you still sitting on that awful thing?
It hasn't hatched yet, and I'm worried it never will.
I might be half blind, but that ain't no duck egg.
That there's a turkey egg!
I wouldn't bother trying to hatch it.
Too late! It's opening!

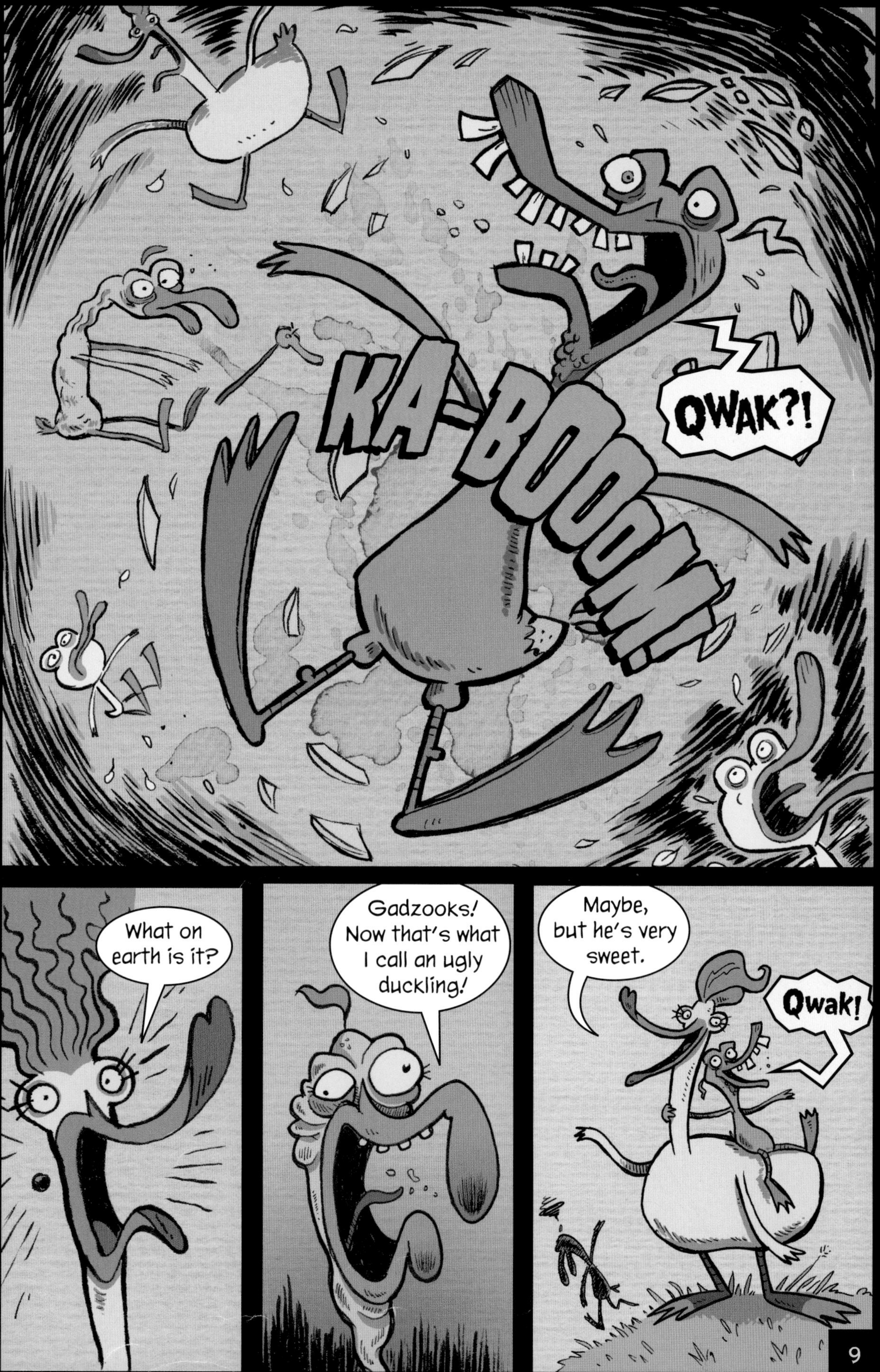
KA-BOOOM!
QWAK?!
What on earth is it?
Gadzooks! Now that's what I call an ugly duckling!
Maybe, but he's very sweet.
Qwak!

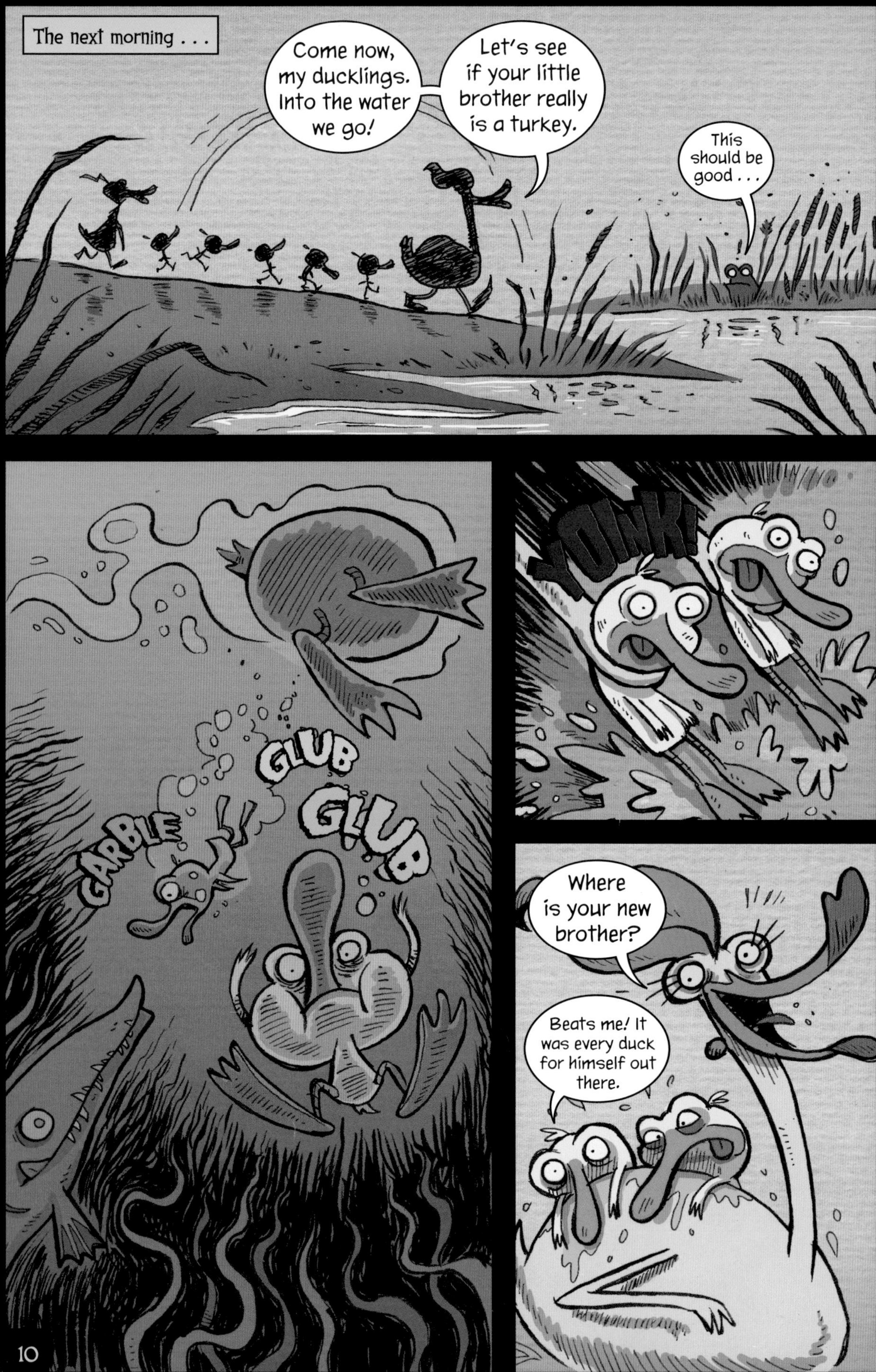

The next morning . . .
Come now, my ducklings. Into the water we go!
Let's see if your little brother really is a turkey.
This should be good . . .
YOINK!
GLUB
GLUB
GARBLE
Where is your new brother?
Beats me! It was every duck for himself out there.

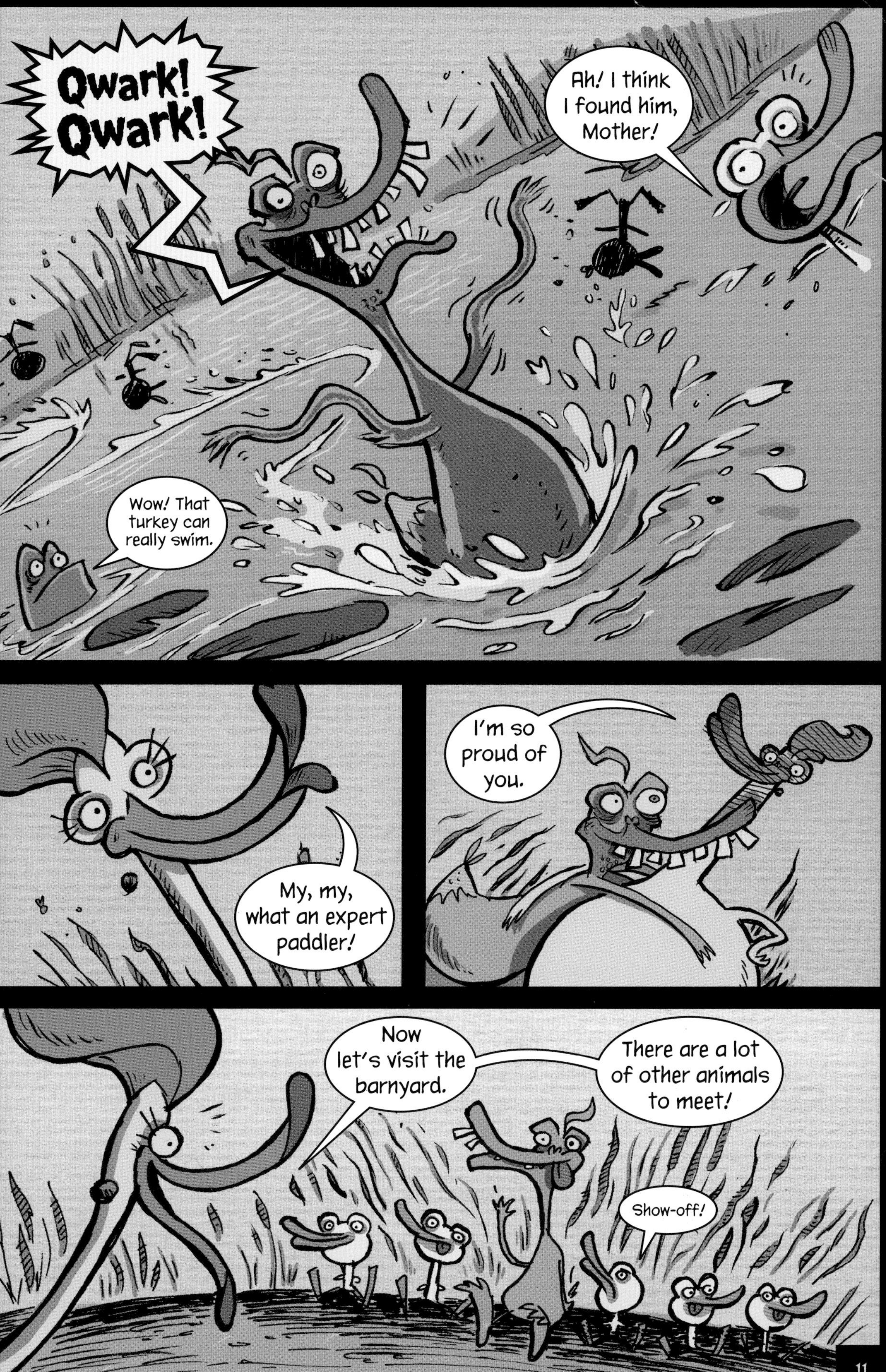
Qwark! Qwark!
Ah! I think I found him, Mother!
Wow! That turkey can really swim.
My, my, what an expert paddler!
I'm so proud of you.
Now let's visit the barnyard.
There are a lot of other animals to meet!
Show-off!

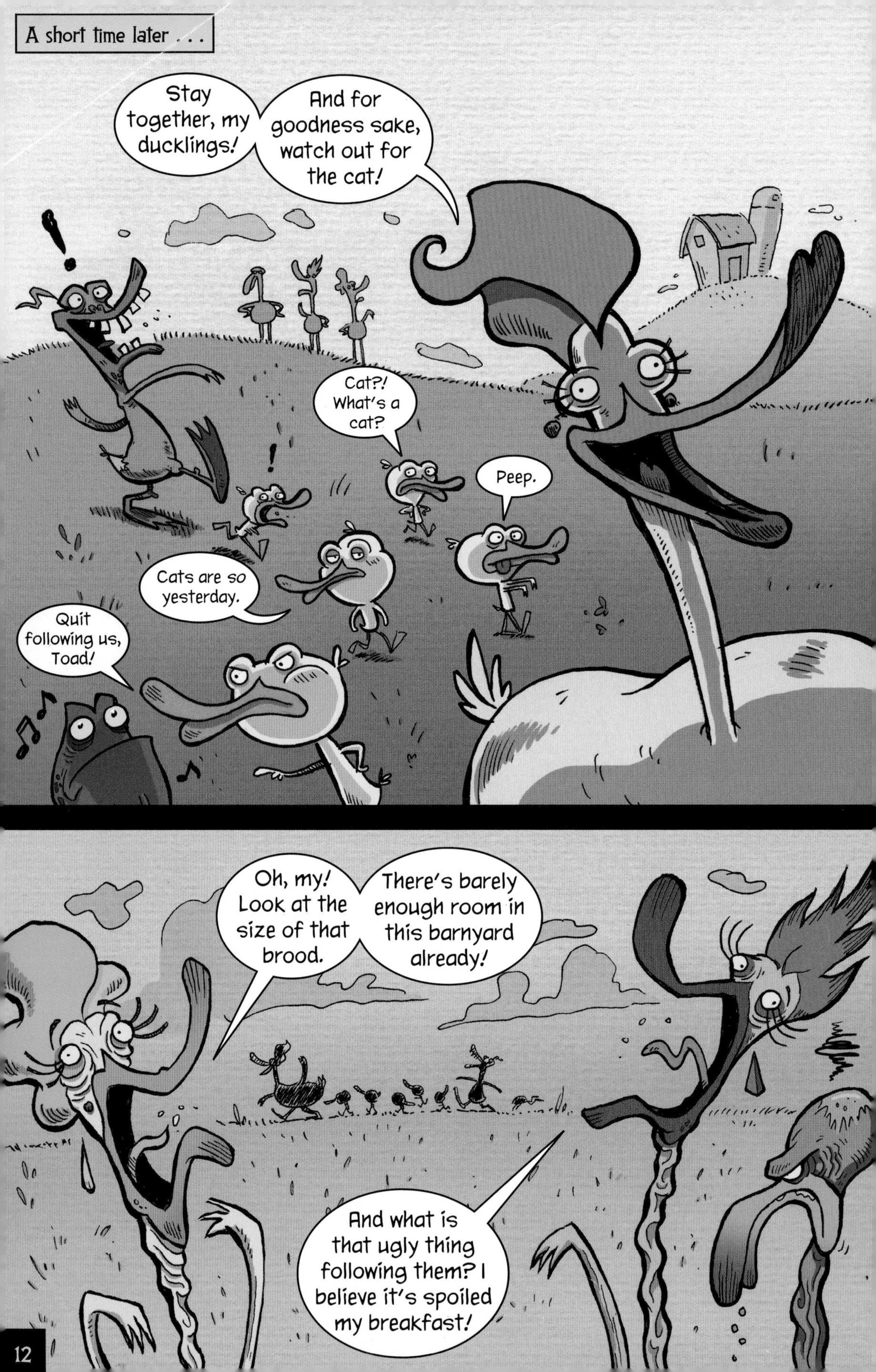
A short time later . . .
Stay together, my ducklings!
And for goodness sake, watch out for the cat!
Cat?! What's a cat?
Peep.
Cats are so yesterday.
Quit following us, Toad!
Oh, my! Look at the size of that brood.
There's barely enough room in this barnyard already!
And what is that ugly thing following them? I believe it's spoiled my breakfast!

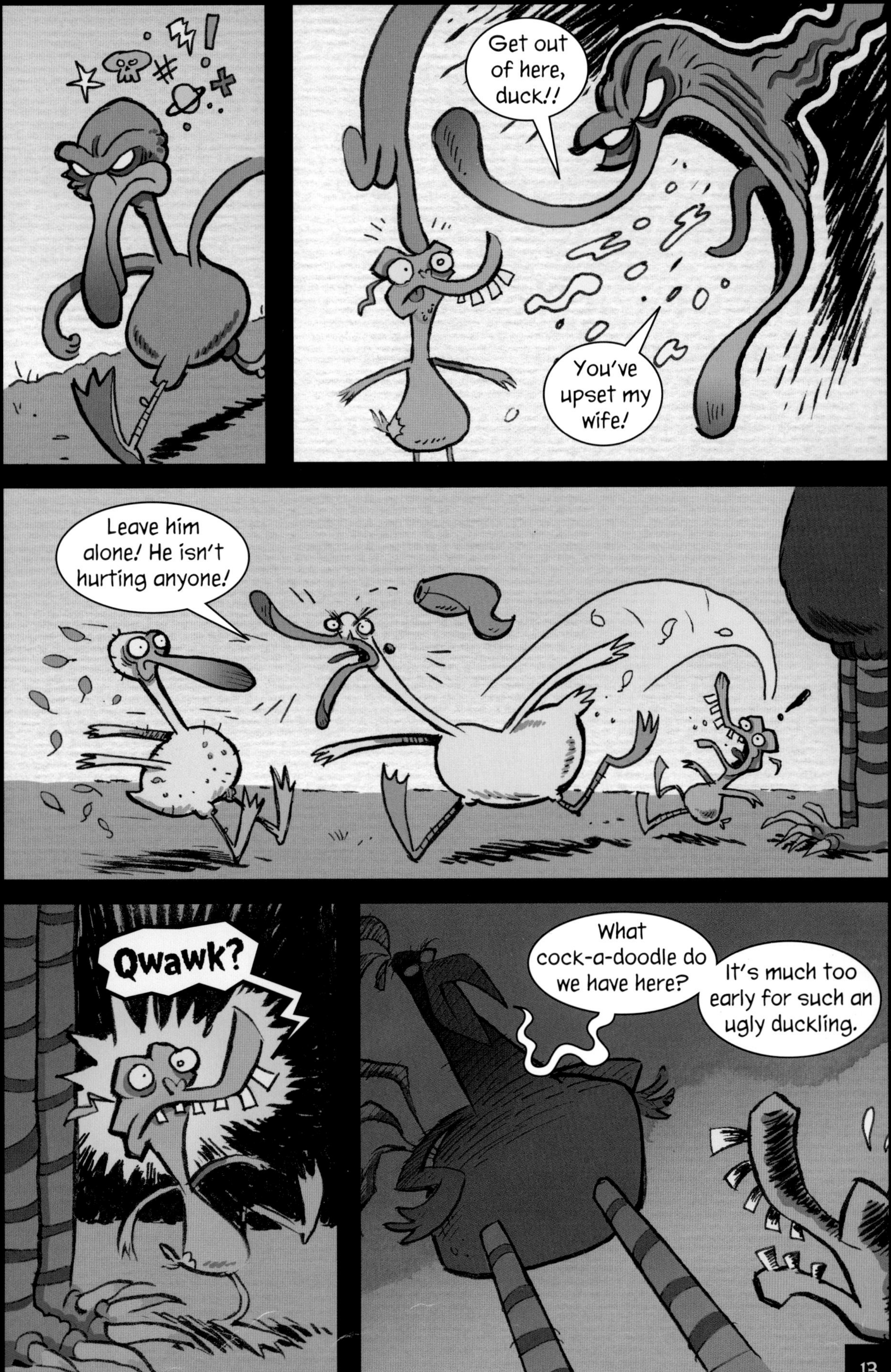
Get out of here, duck!!
You've upset my wife!
Leave him alone! He isn't hurting anyone!
Qwawk?
What cock-a-doodle do we have here?
It's much too early for such an ugly duckling.

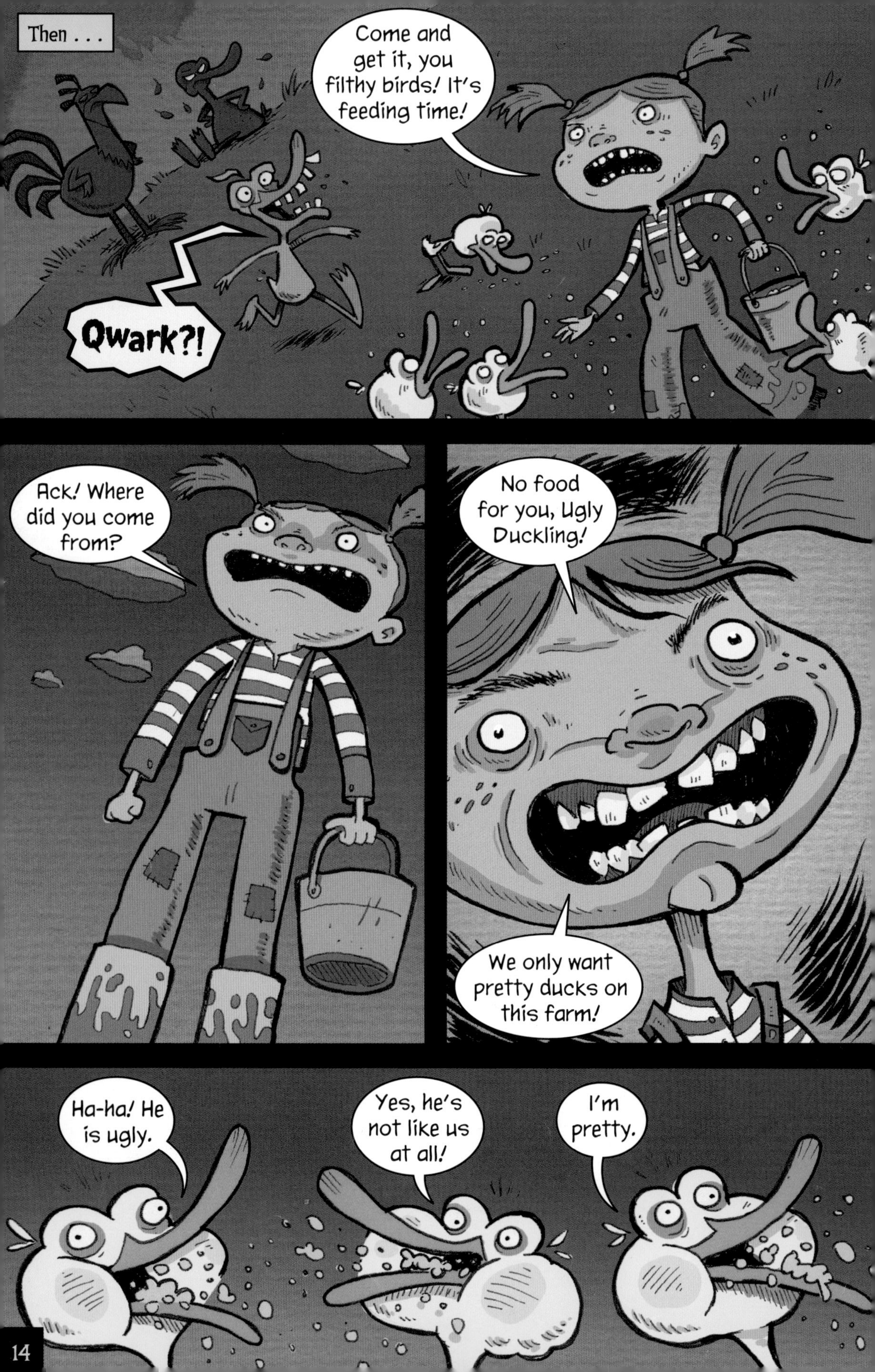
Then . . .
Come and get it, you filthy birds! It's feeding time!
Qwark?!
Ack! Where did you come from?
No food for you, Ugly Duckling!
We only want pretty ducks on this farm!
Ha-ha! He is ugly.
Yes, he's not like us at all!
I'm pretty.

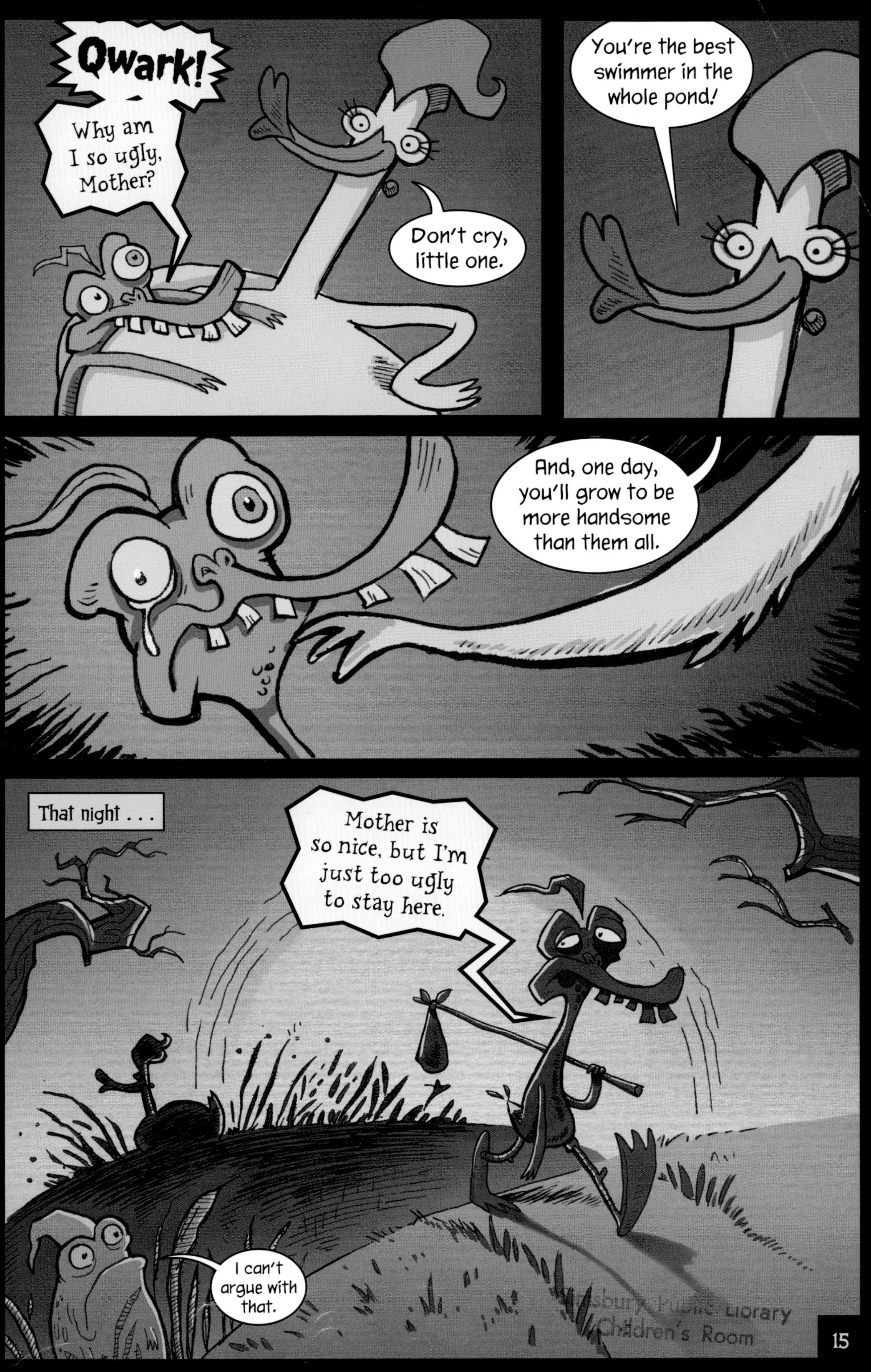
Qwark!
Why am I so ugly, Mother?
Don't cry, little one.
You're the best swimmer in the whole pond!
And, one day, you'll grow to be more handsome than them all.
That night . . .
Mother is so nice, but I'm just too ugly to stay here.
I can't argue with that.

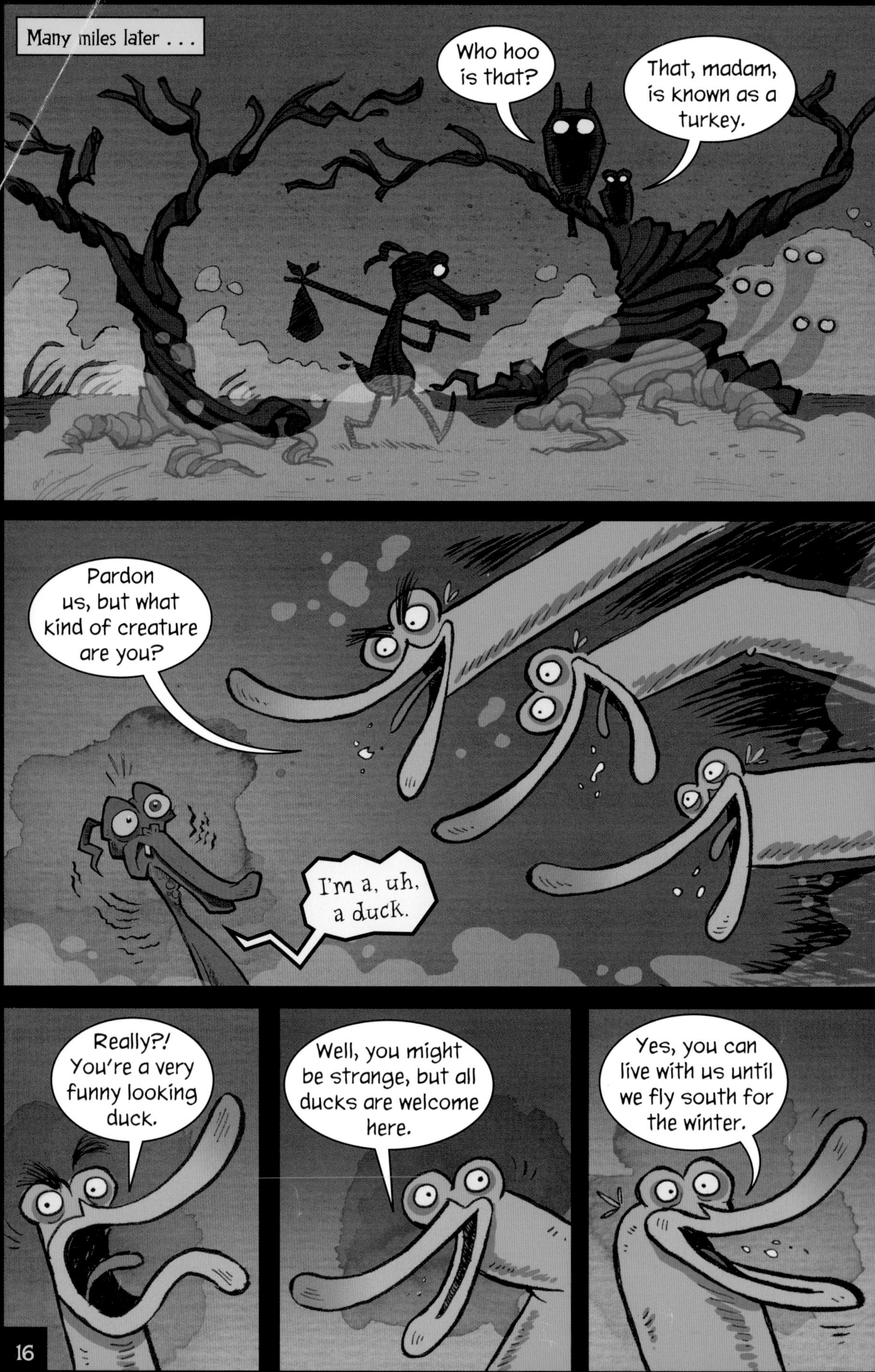

Many miles later . . .
Who hoo is that?
That, madam, is known as a turkey.
Pardon us, but what kind of creature are you?
I'm a, uh, a duck.
Really?! You're a very funny looking duck.
Well, you might be strange, but all ducks are welcome here.
Yes, you can live with us until we fly south for the winter.

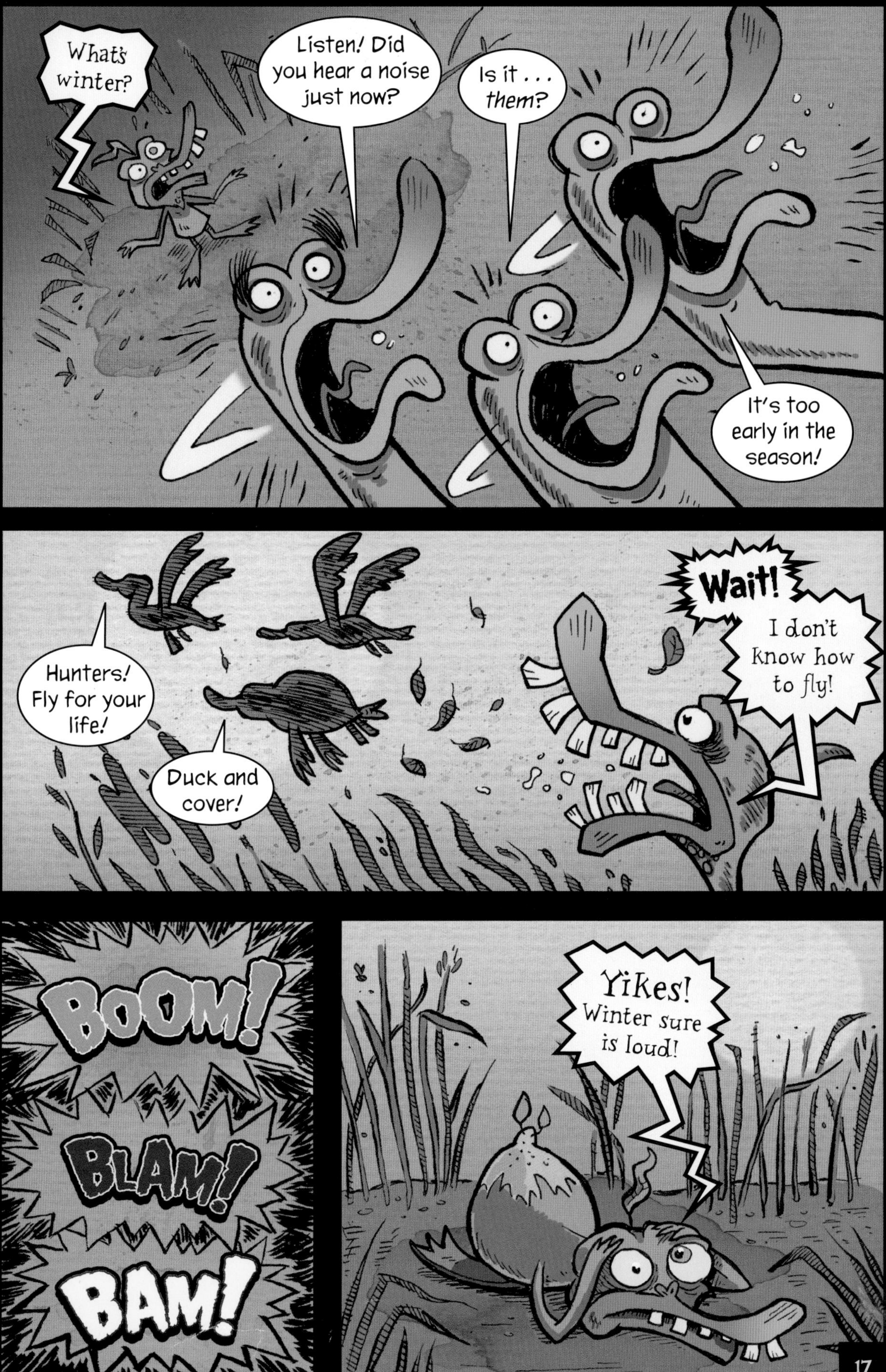
What's winter?
Listen! Did you hear a noise just now?
Is it . . . *them*?
It's too early in the season!
Hunters! Fly for your life!
Duck and cover!
Wait!
I don't know how to *fly*!
BOOM!
BLAM!
BAM!
Yikes! Winter sure is loud!

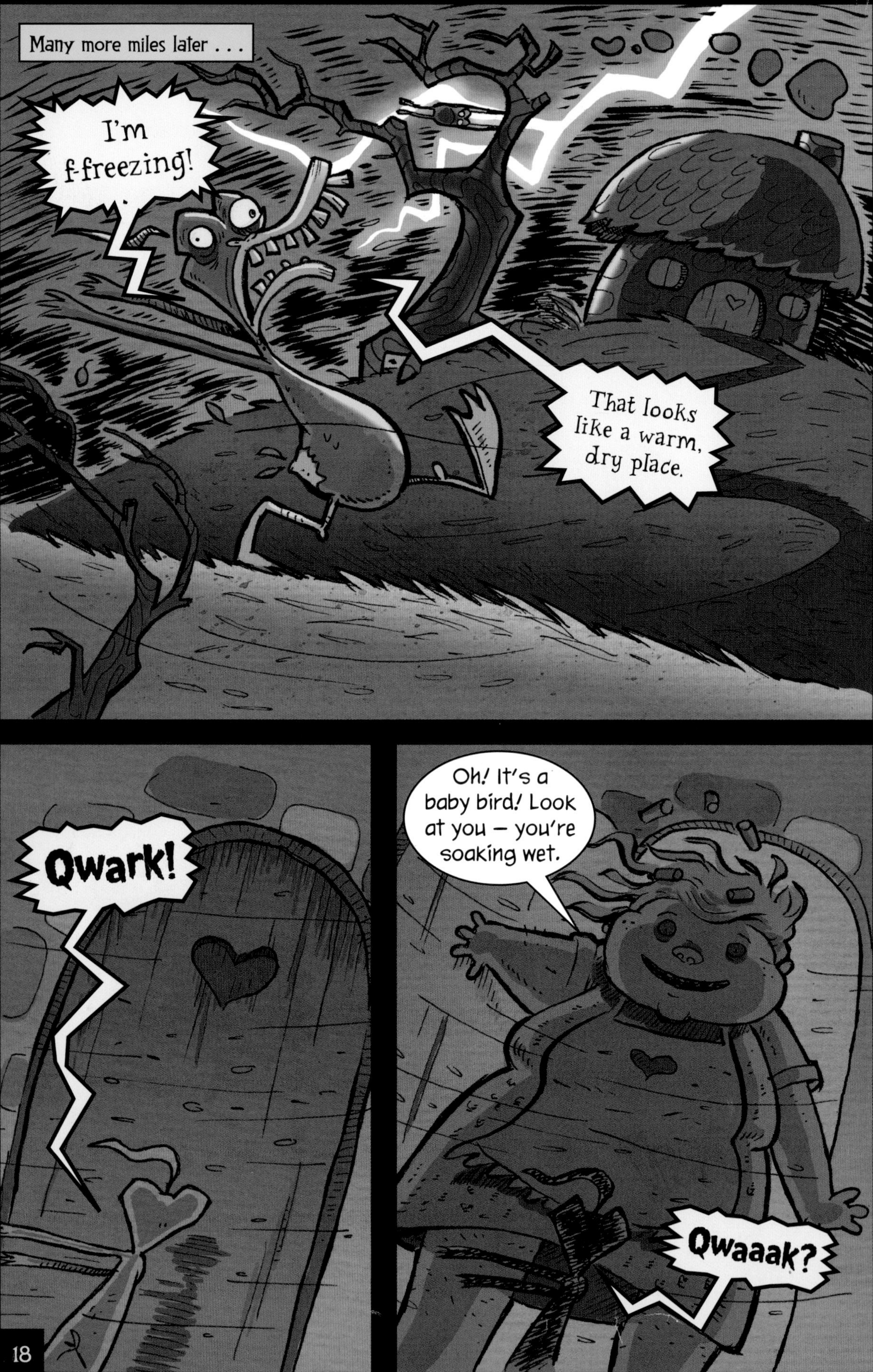
Many more miles later . . .
I'm f-freezing!
That looks like a warm, dry place.
Qwark!
Oh! It's a baby bird! Look at you — you're soaking wet.
Qwaaak?

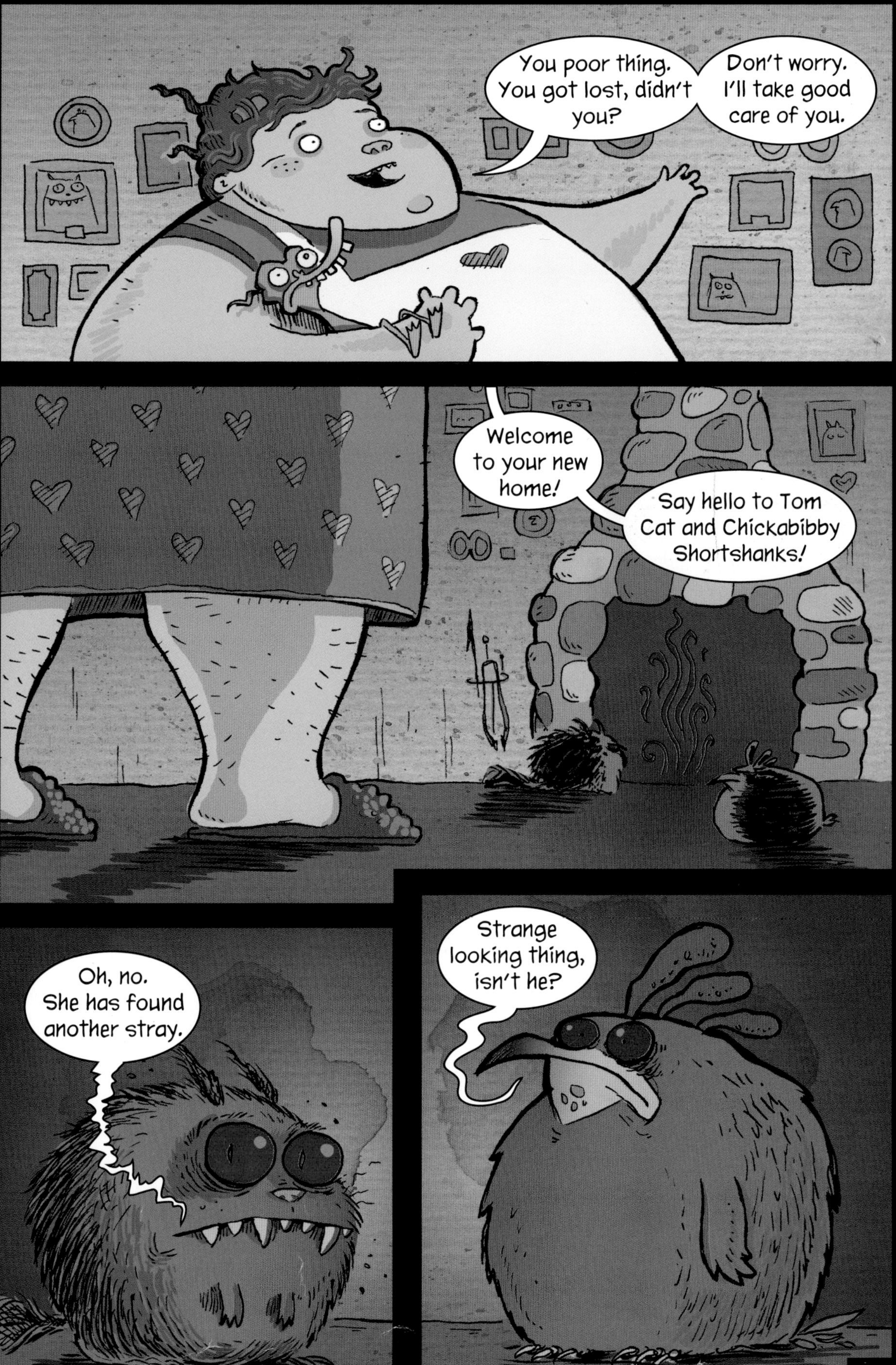

You poor thing. You got lost, didn't you?
Don't worry. I'll take good care of you.
Welcome to your new home!
Say hello to Tom Cat and Chickabibby Shortshanks!
Oh, no. She has found another stray.
Strange looking thing, isn't he?

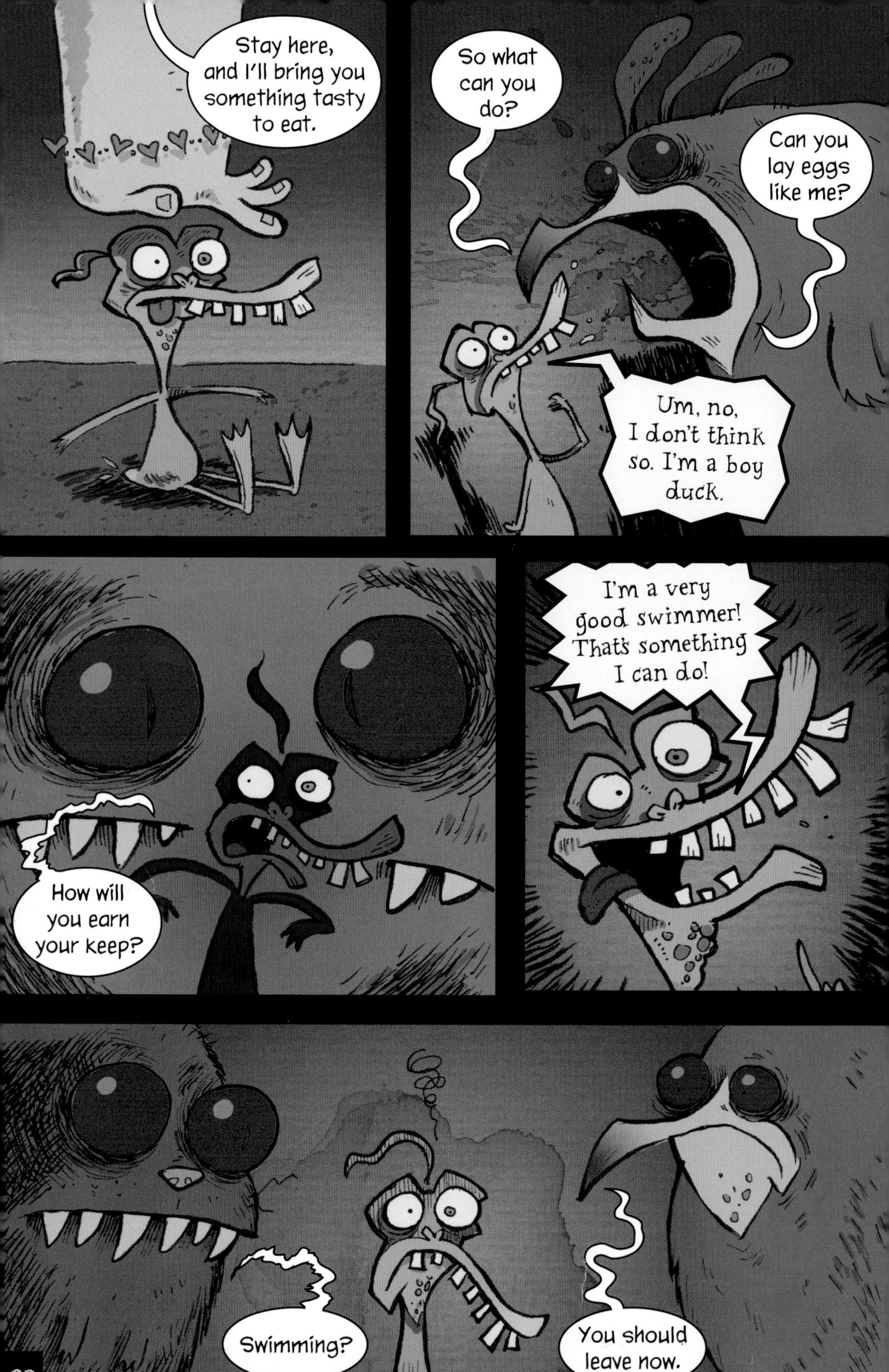
Stay here, and I'll bring you something tasty to eat.
So what can you do?
Can you lay eggs like me?
Um, no, I don't think so. I'm a boy duck.
How will you earn your keep?
I'm a very good swimmer! That's something I can do!
Swimming?
You should leave now.

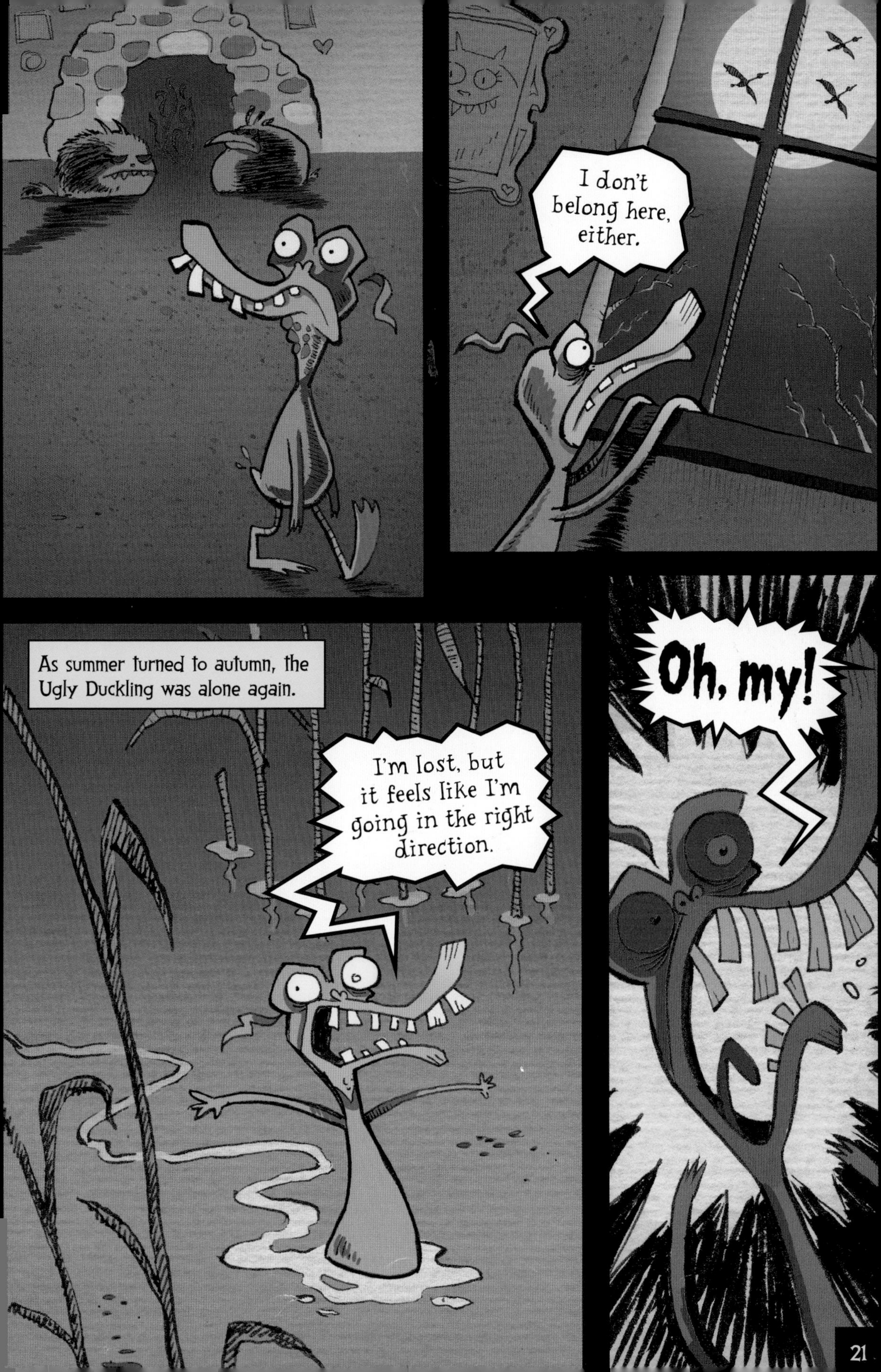
I don't belong here, either.
As summer turned to autumn, the Ugly Duckling was alone again.
I'm lost, but it feels like I'm going in the right direction.
Oh, my!

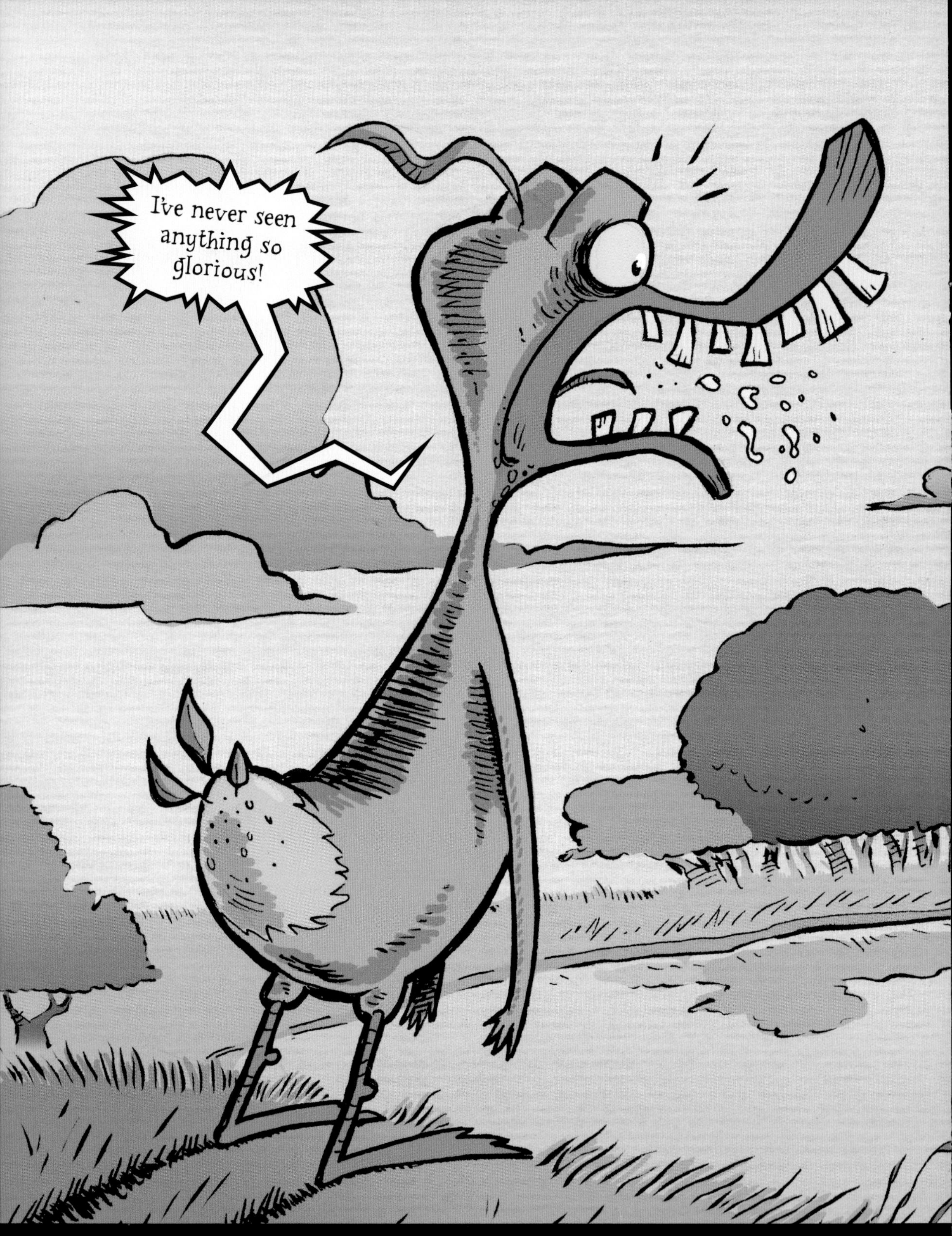
I've never seen anything so glorious!

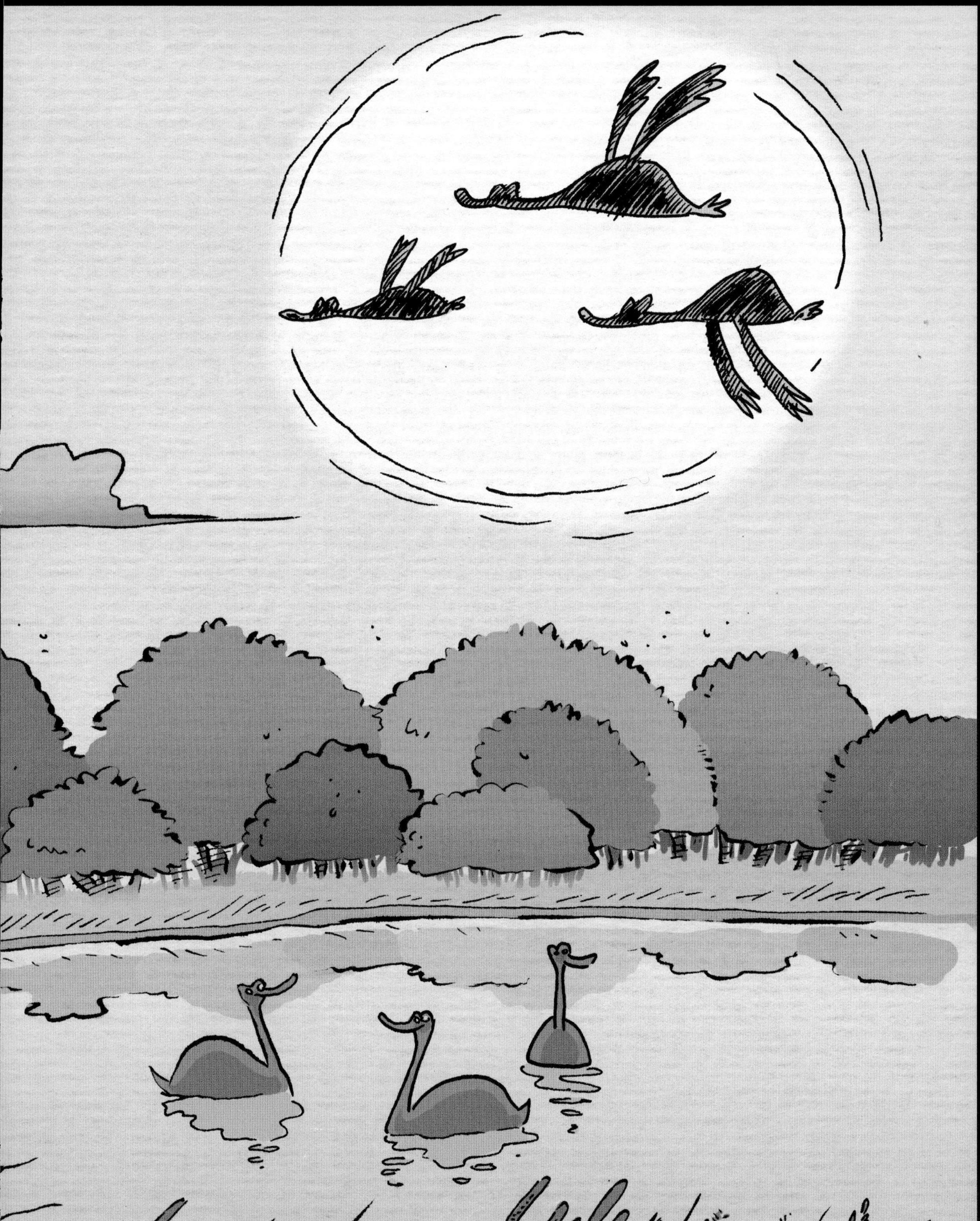

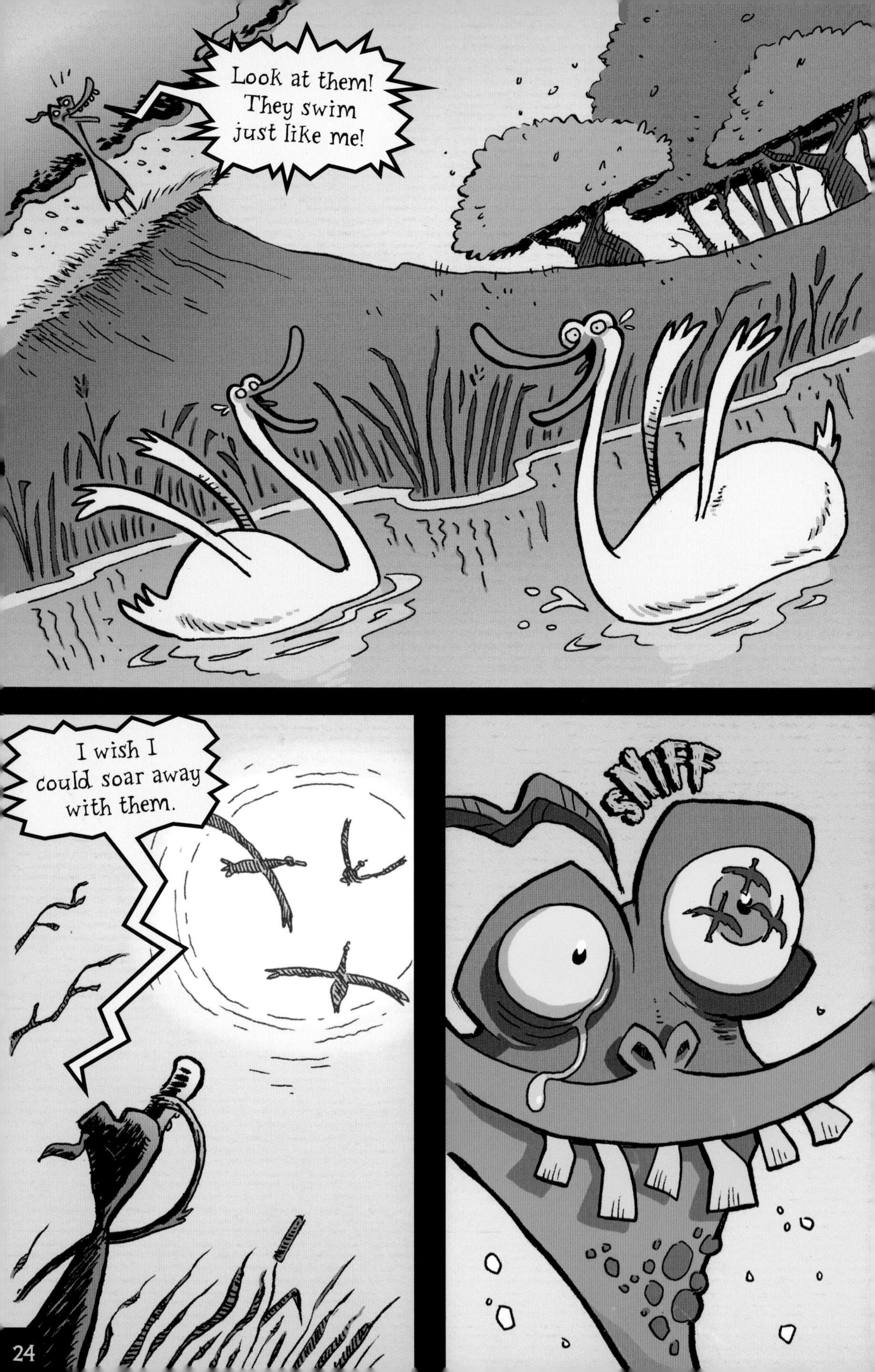
Look at them! They swim just like me!
I wish I could soar away with them.
SNIFF

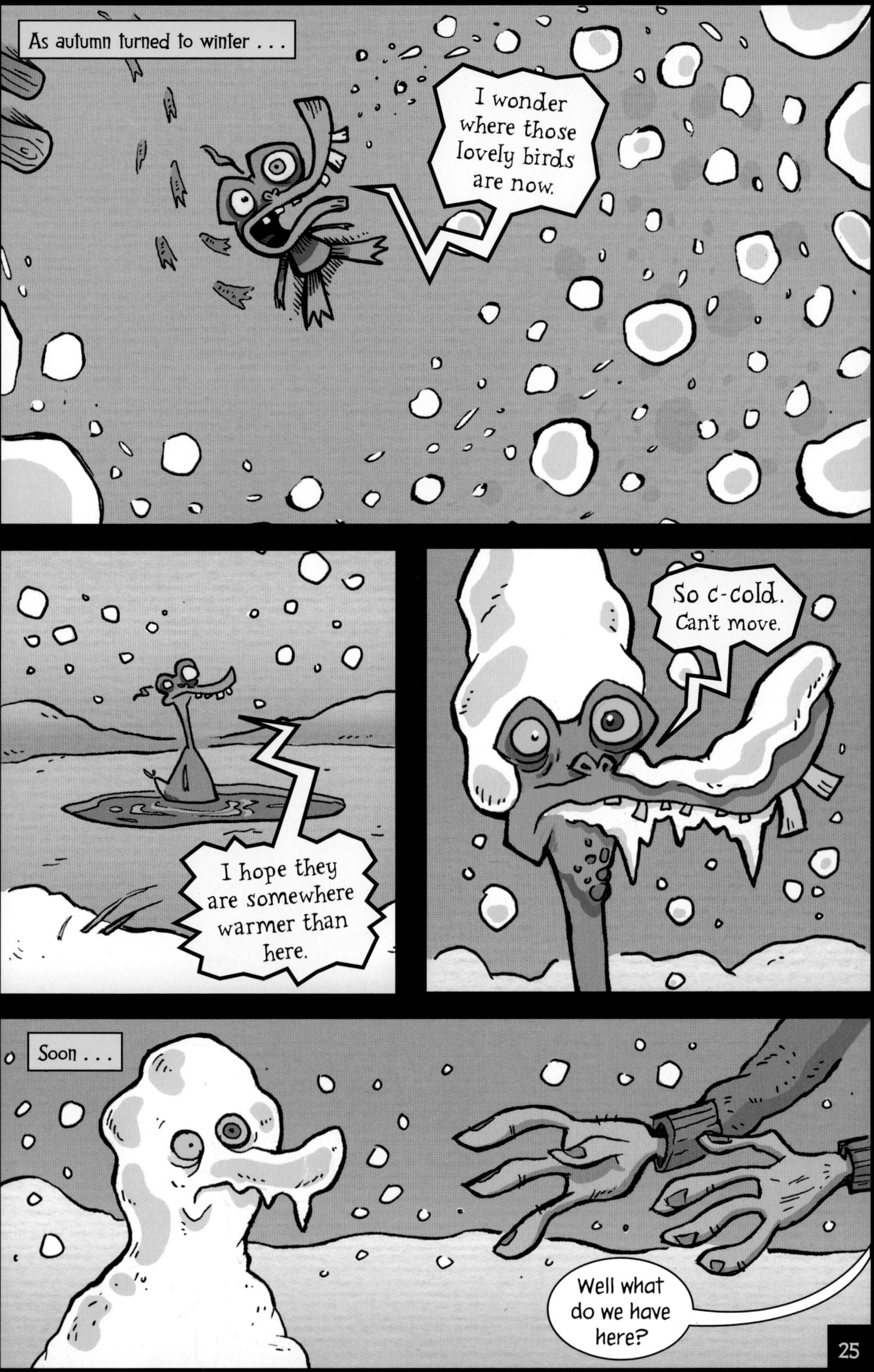
As autumn turned to winter . . .
I wonder where those lovely birds are now.
I hope they are somewhere warmer than here.
So c-cold. Can't move.
Soon . . .
Well what do we have here?

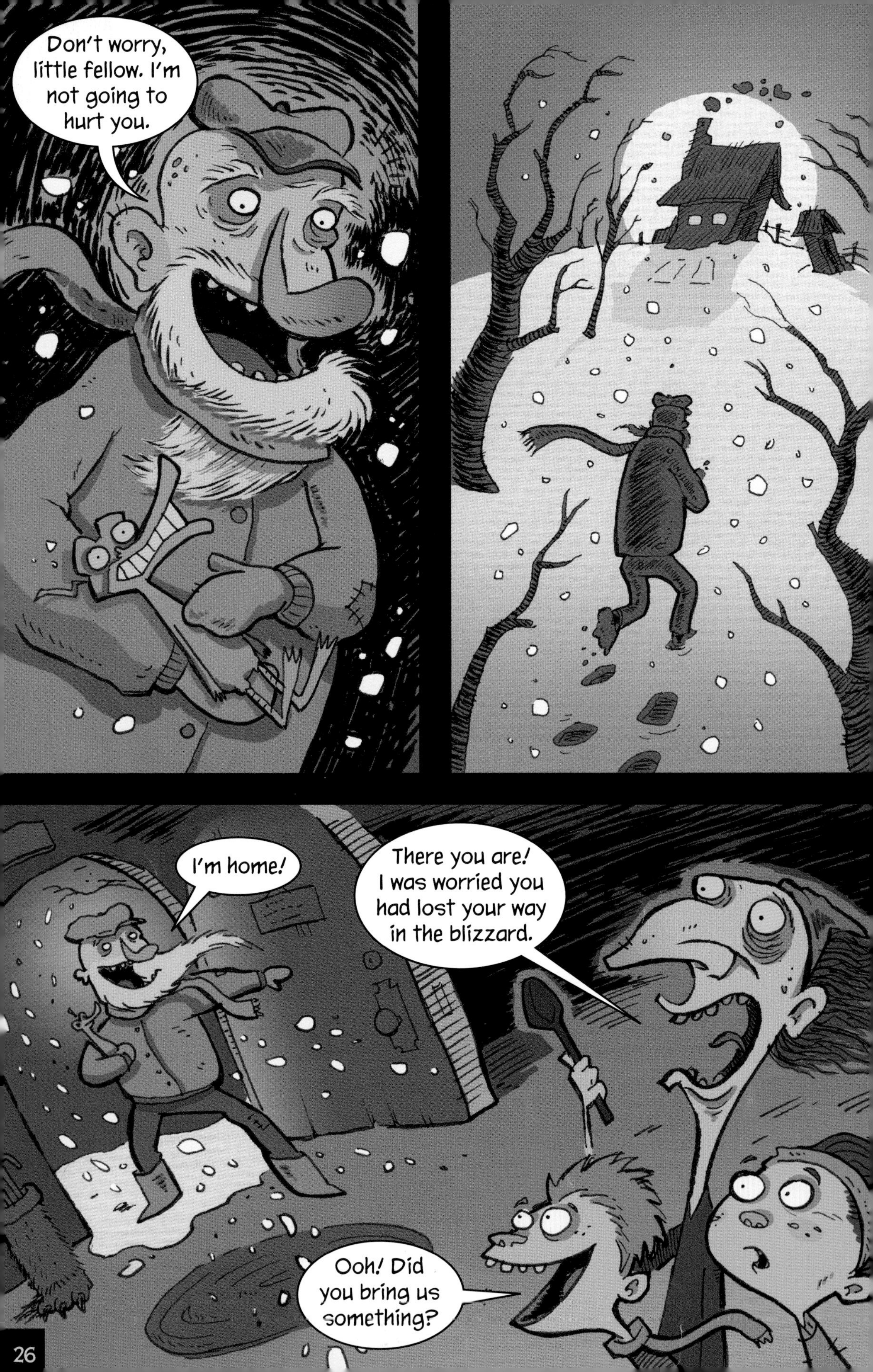
Don't worry, little fellow. I'm not going to hurt you.
I'm home!
There you are! I was worried you had lost your way in the blizzard.
Ooh! Did you bring us something?

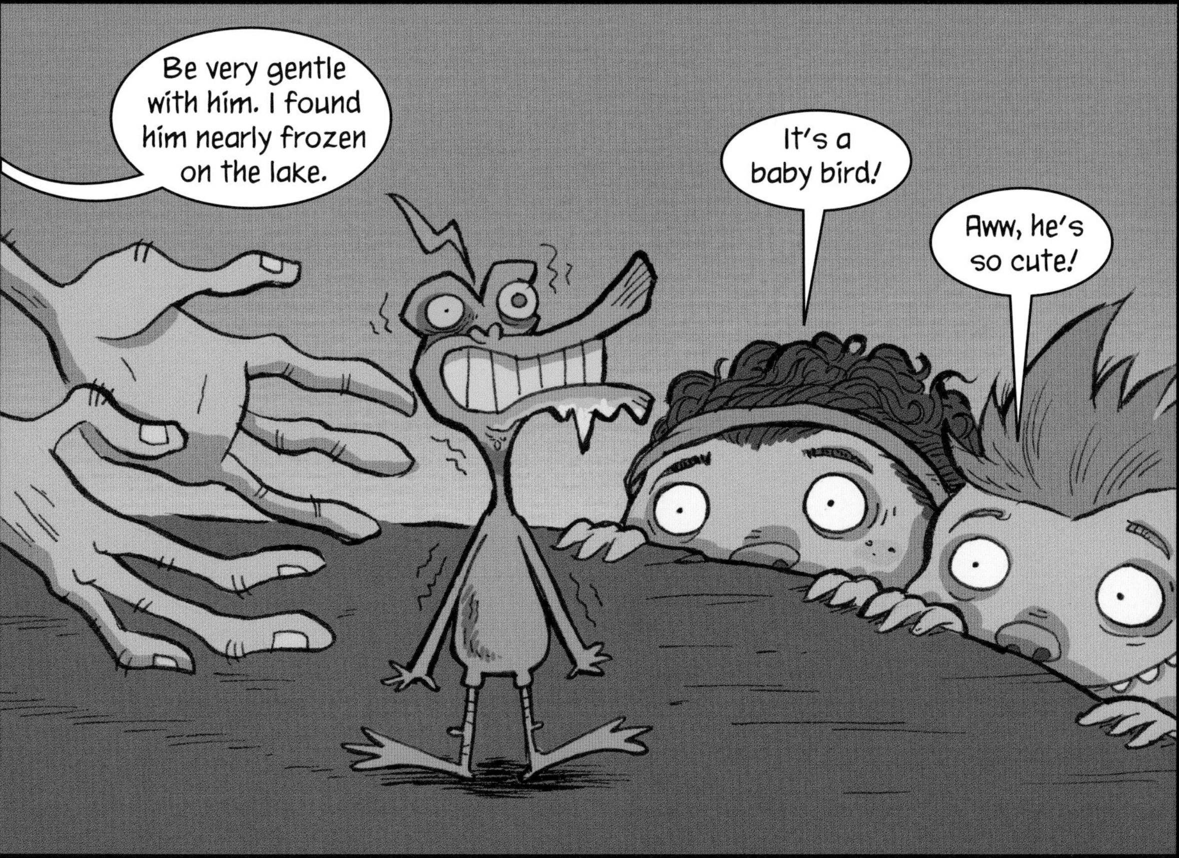
Be very gentle with him. I found him nearly frozen on the lake.
It's a baby bird!
Aww, he's so cute!

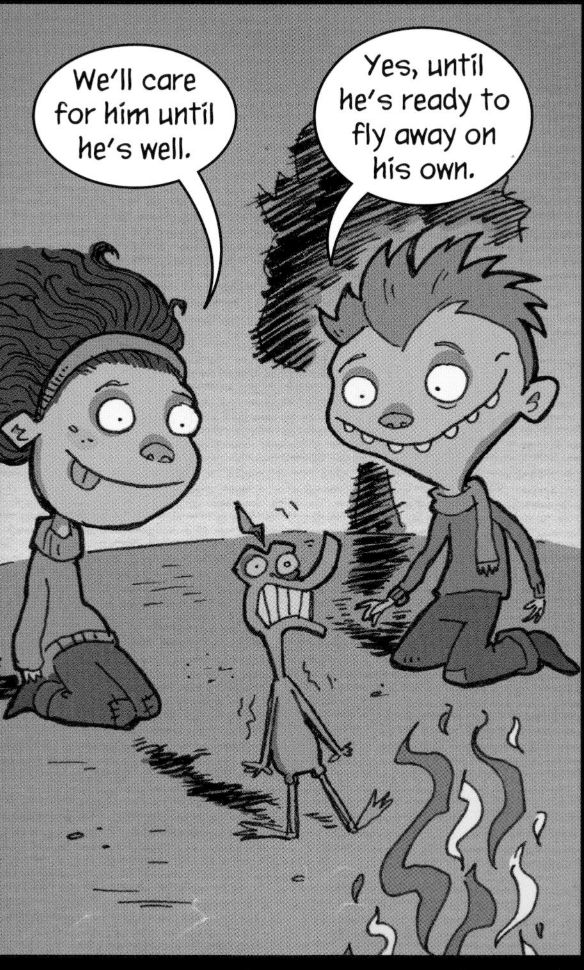
We'll care for him until he's well.
Yes, until he's ready to fly away on his own.

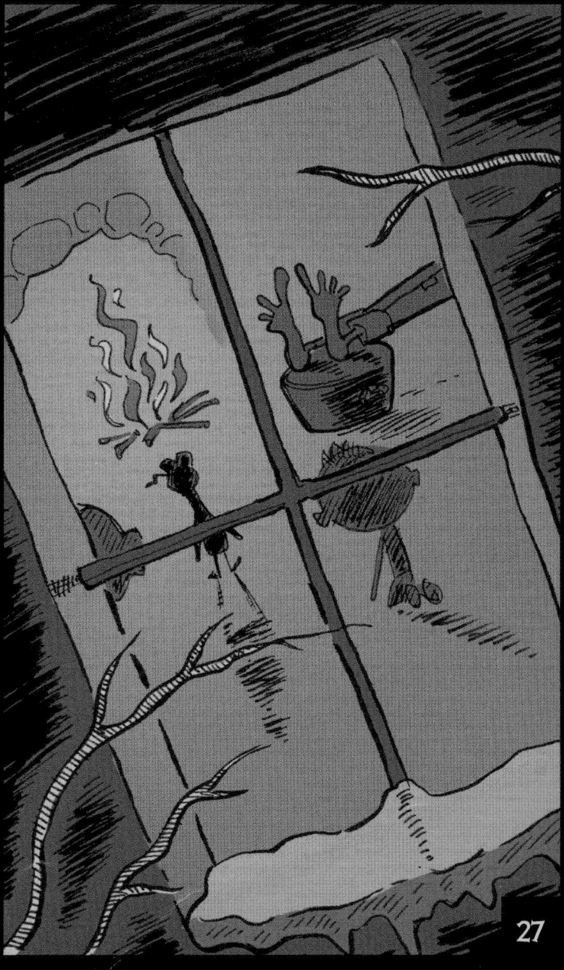

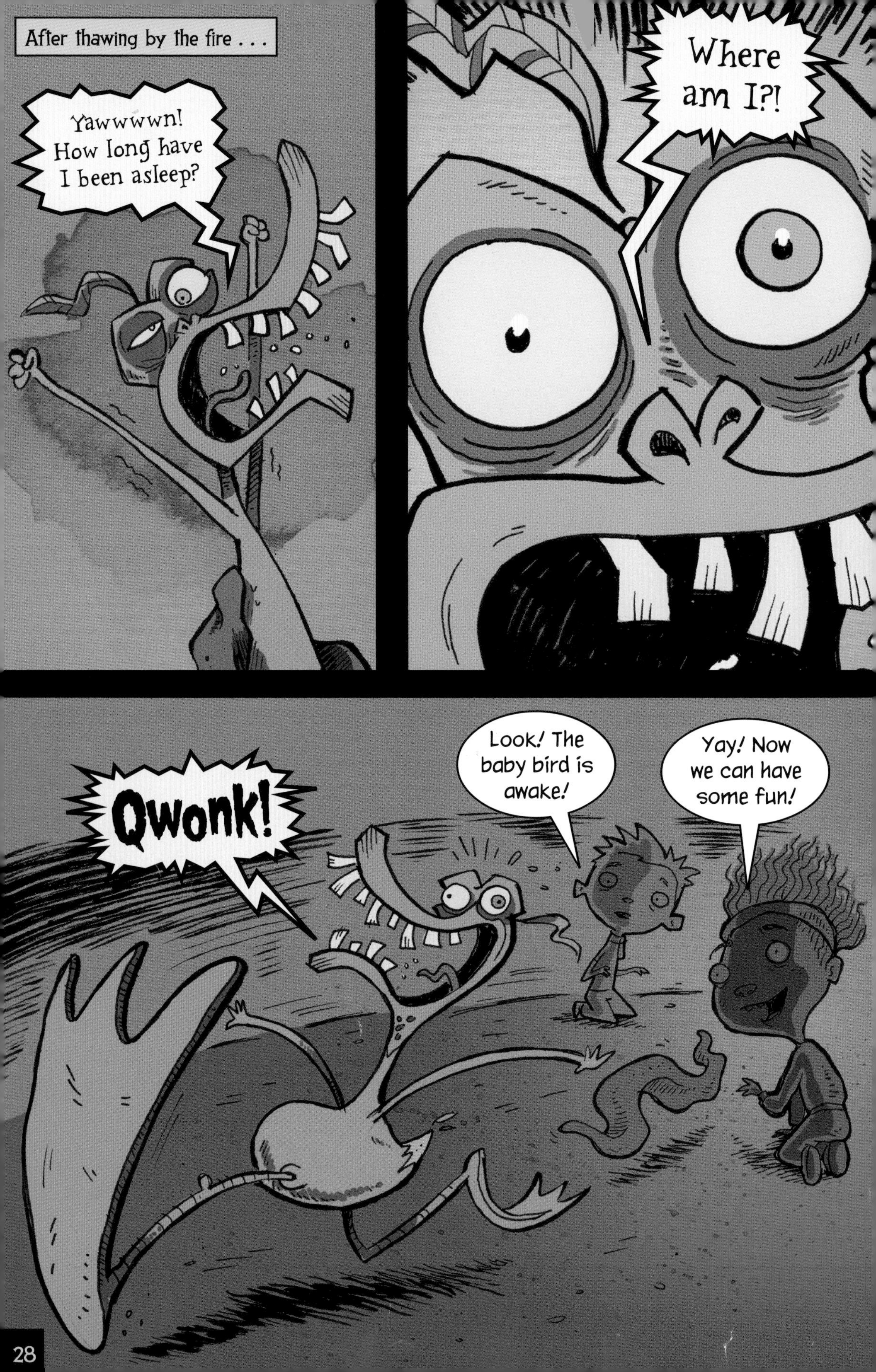
After thawing by the fire . . .
Yawwwwn! How long have I been asleep?
Where am I?!
Qwonk!
Look! The baby bird is awake!
Yay! Now we can have some fun!

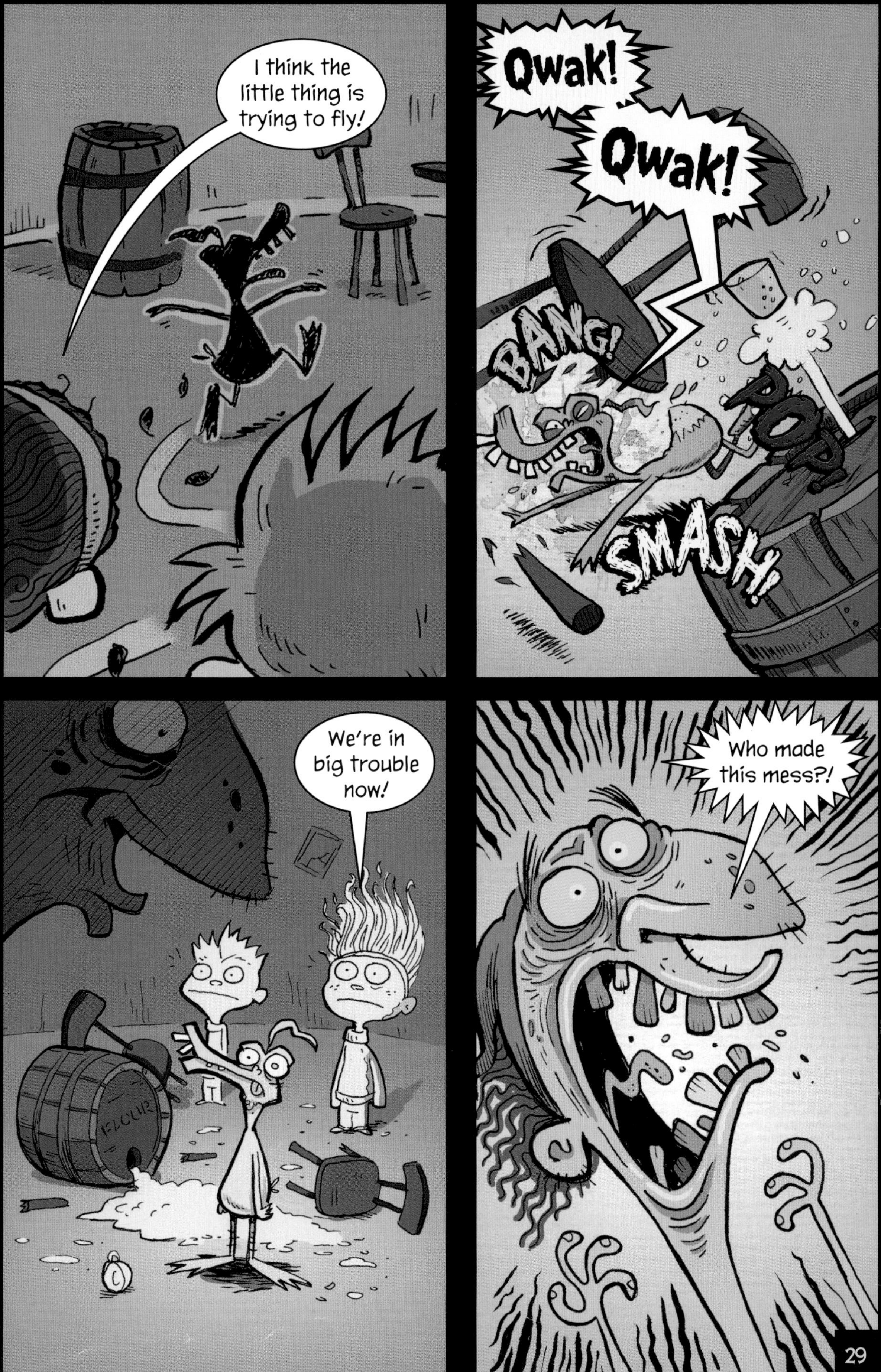

I think the little thing is trying to fly!
Qwak!
Qwak!
BANG!
POP!
SMASH!
We're in big trouble now!
FLOUR
Who made this mess?!

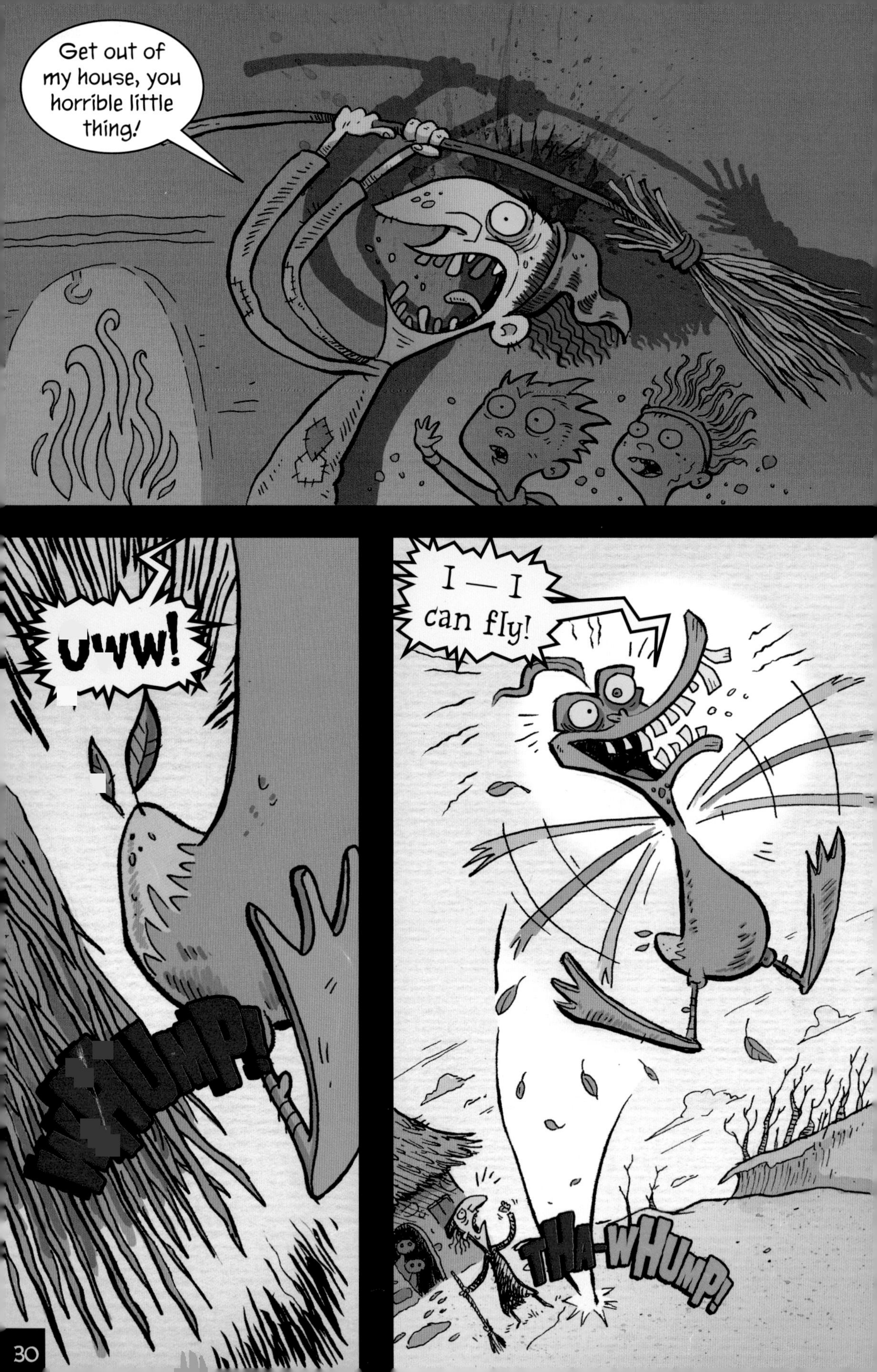
Get out of my house, you horrible little thing!
I — I can fly!
THA-WHUMP!

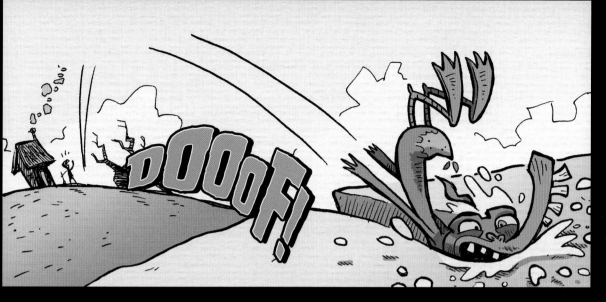

Later...

FLUTTER FLUTTER

Show-off.

The Ugly Duckling went back to the lake...

...and found that, like the seasons, he too had changed.

Is that... me?

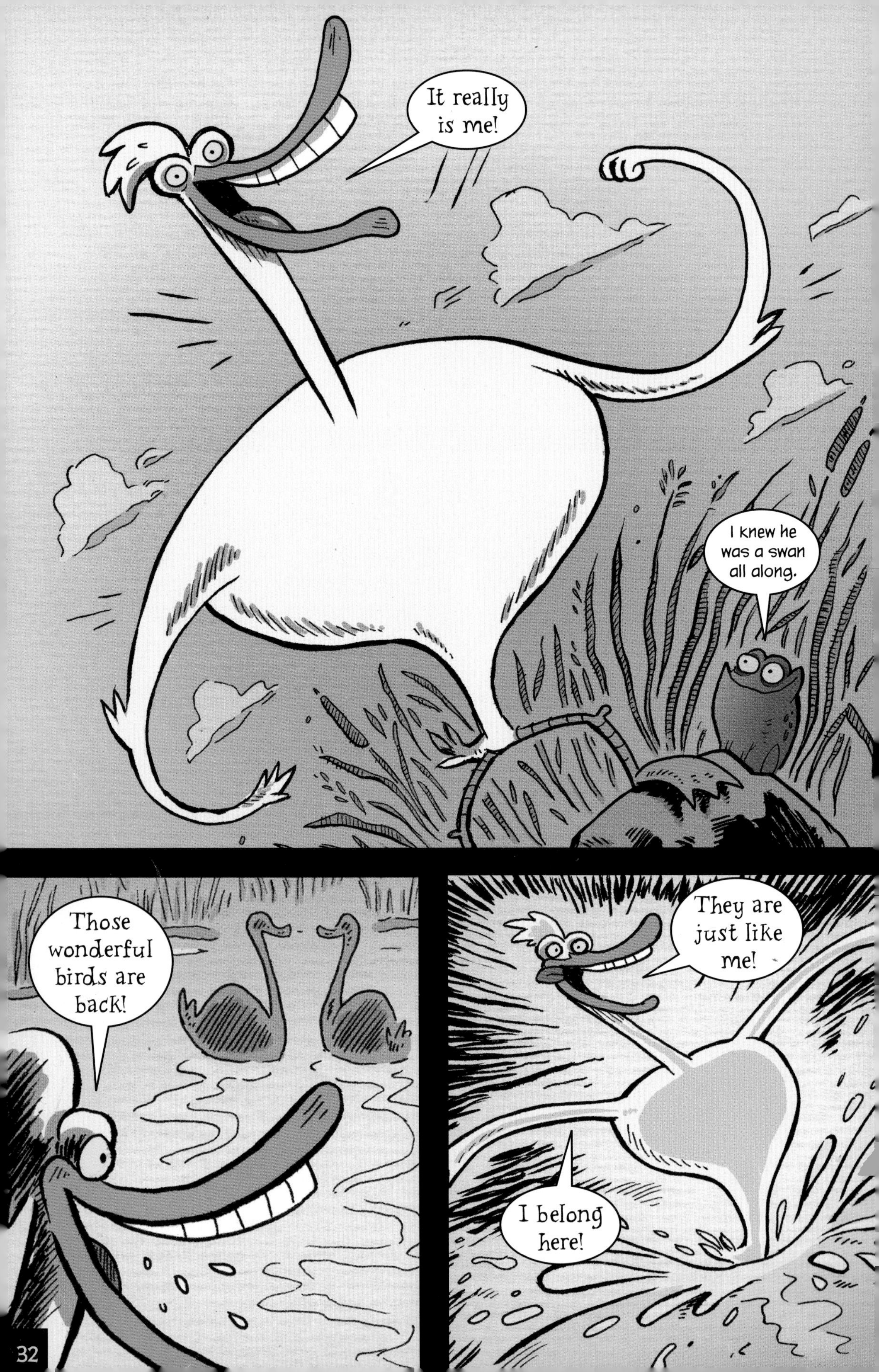
It really is me!
I knew he was a swan all along.
Those wonderful birds are back!
They are just like me!
I belong here!

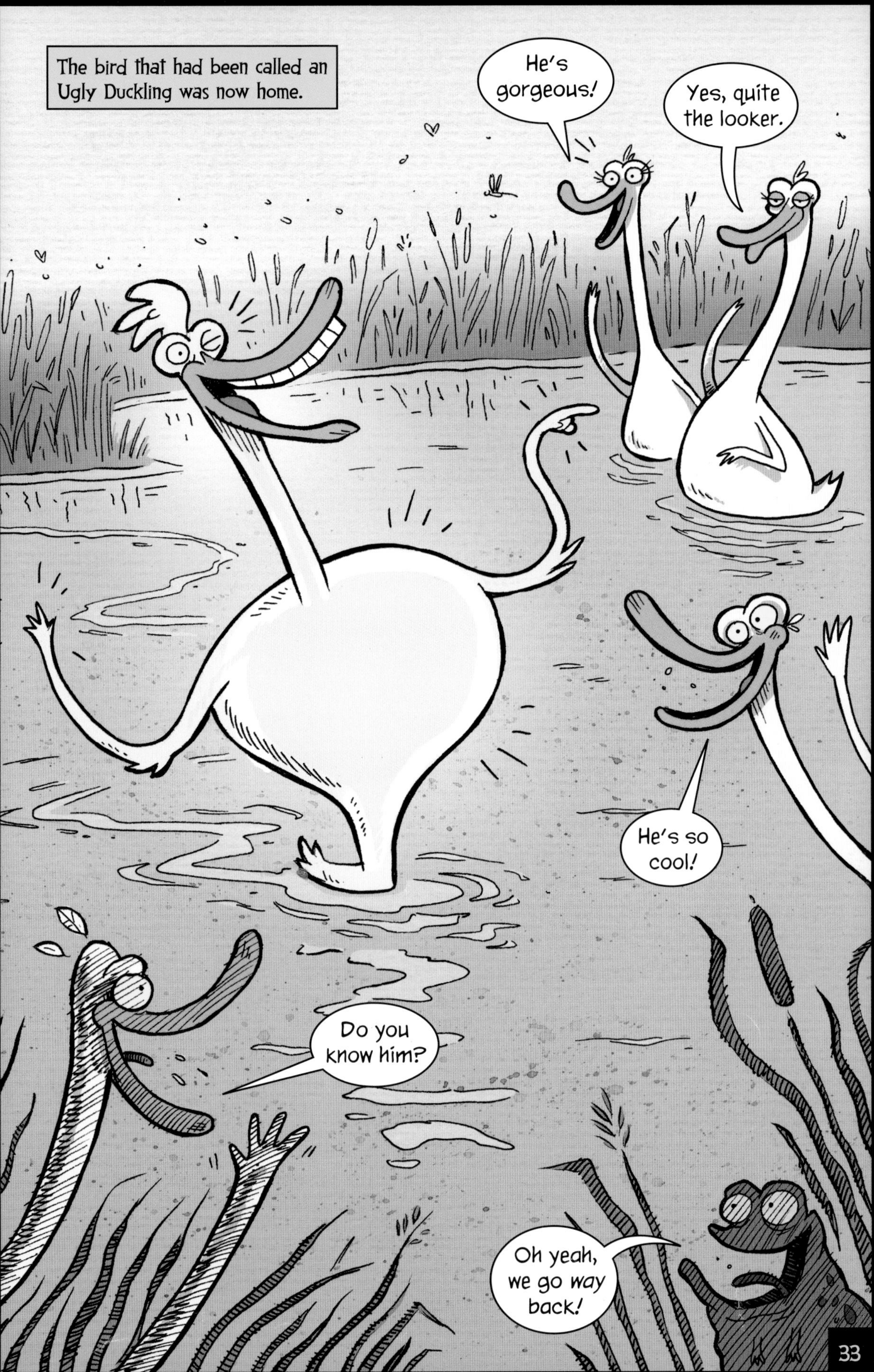
The bird that had been called an Ugly Duckling was now home.
He's gorgeous!
Yes, quite the looker.
He's so cool!
Do you know him?
Oh yeah, we go way back!

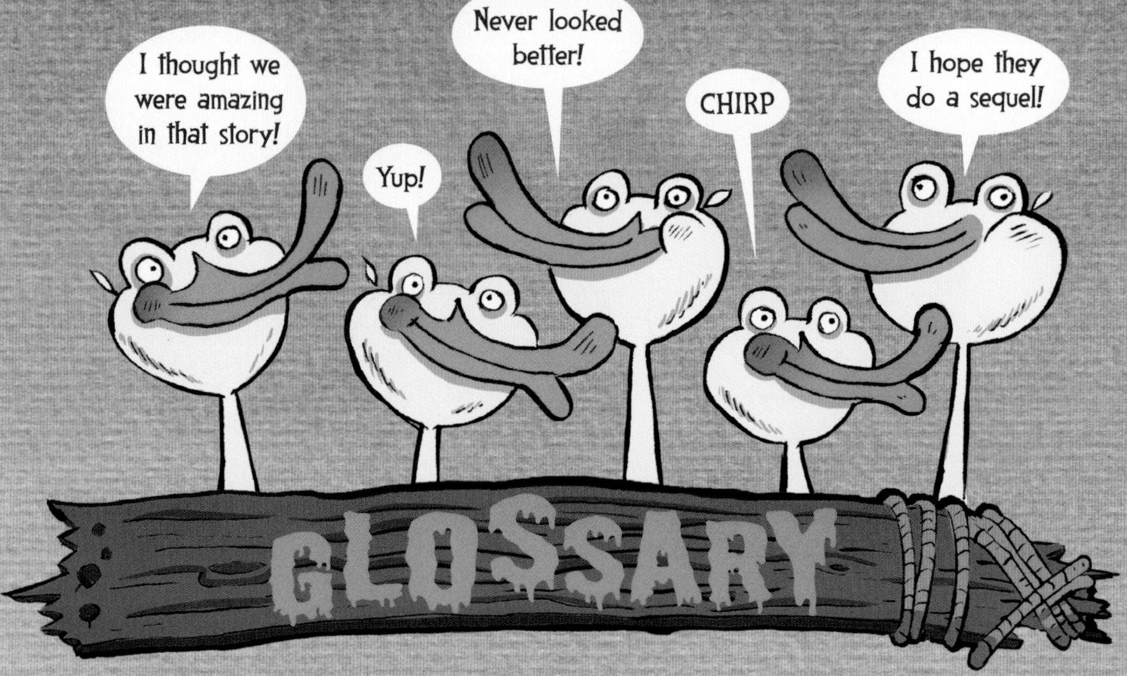
I thought we were amazing in that story!
Yup!
Never looked better!
CHIRP
I hope they do a sequel!
GLOSSARY

brood (BROOD)—a family of young birds, or all the children in a family

expert (EK-spurt)—very skilled at something

gentle (JEN-tuhl)—kind or sensitive

glorious (GLOR-ee-uhss)—beautiful and amazing

hatch (HACH)—when an egg hatches, it breaks open and the baby emerges

spoiled (SPOILD)—ruined or wrecked something

stray (STRAY)—a lost animal

THE AUTHOR

HANS CHRISTIAN ANDERSEN

Hans Christian Andersen was born in Odense, Denmark, on April 2, 1805. As Hans grew up, he tried many different professions, but none seemed to fit. He eventually found work as an actor and singer, but when his voice changed, he could no longer sing well enough to make a living. Then a friend suggested that he start writing. A short time later, he published his first story, "The Ghost at Palnatoke's Grave."

Andersen's first book of fairy tales was published in 1835. He continued to write children's stories, publishing one almost every year, until he fell ill in 1872. Andersen had written more than 150 fairy tales before his death in 1875. He is considered to be the father of the modern fairy tale.

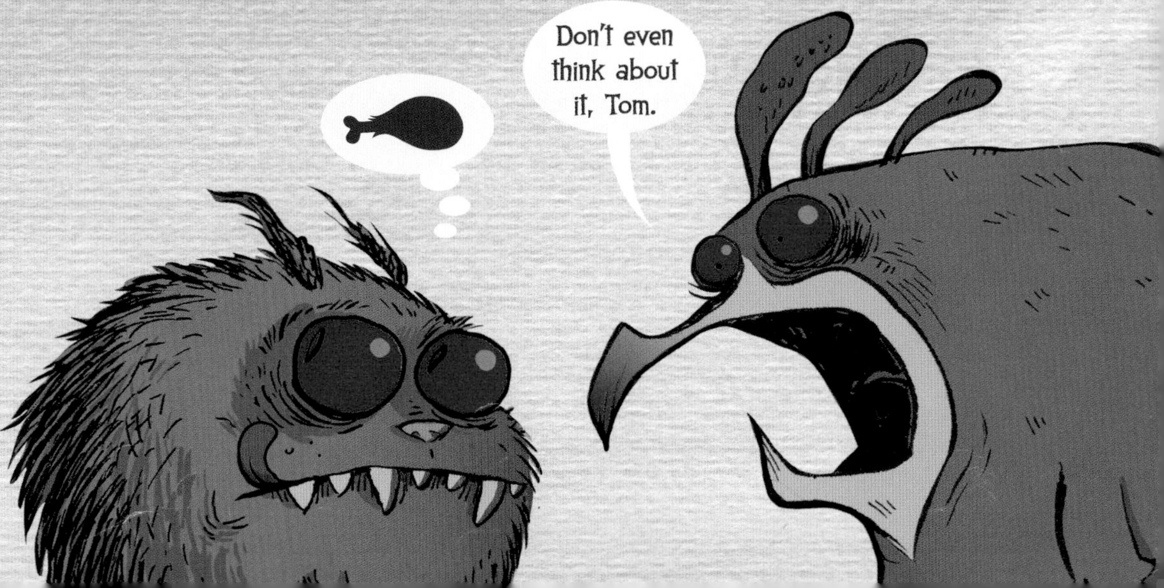
Don't even think about it, Tom.

THE RETELLER

MARTIN POWELL

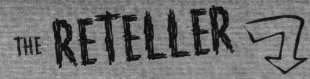

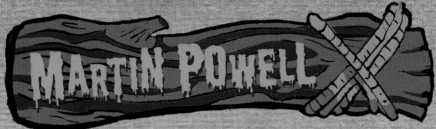

Since 1986, Martin Powell has been a freelance writer. He has written hundreds of stories, many of which have been published by Disney, Marvel, Tekno Comix, Moonstone Books, and others. In 1989, Powell received an Eisner Award nomination for his graphic novel *Scarlet in Gaslight*. This award is one of the highest comic book honors.

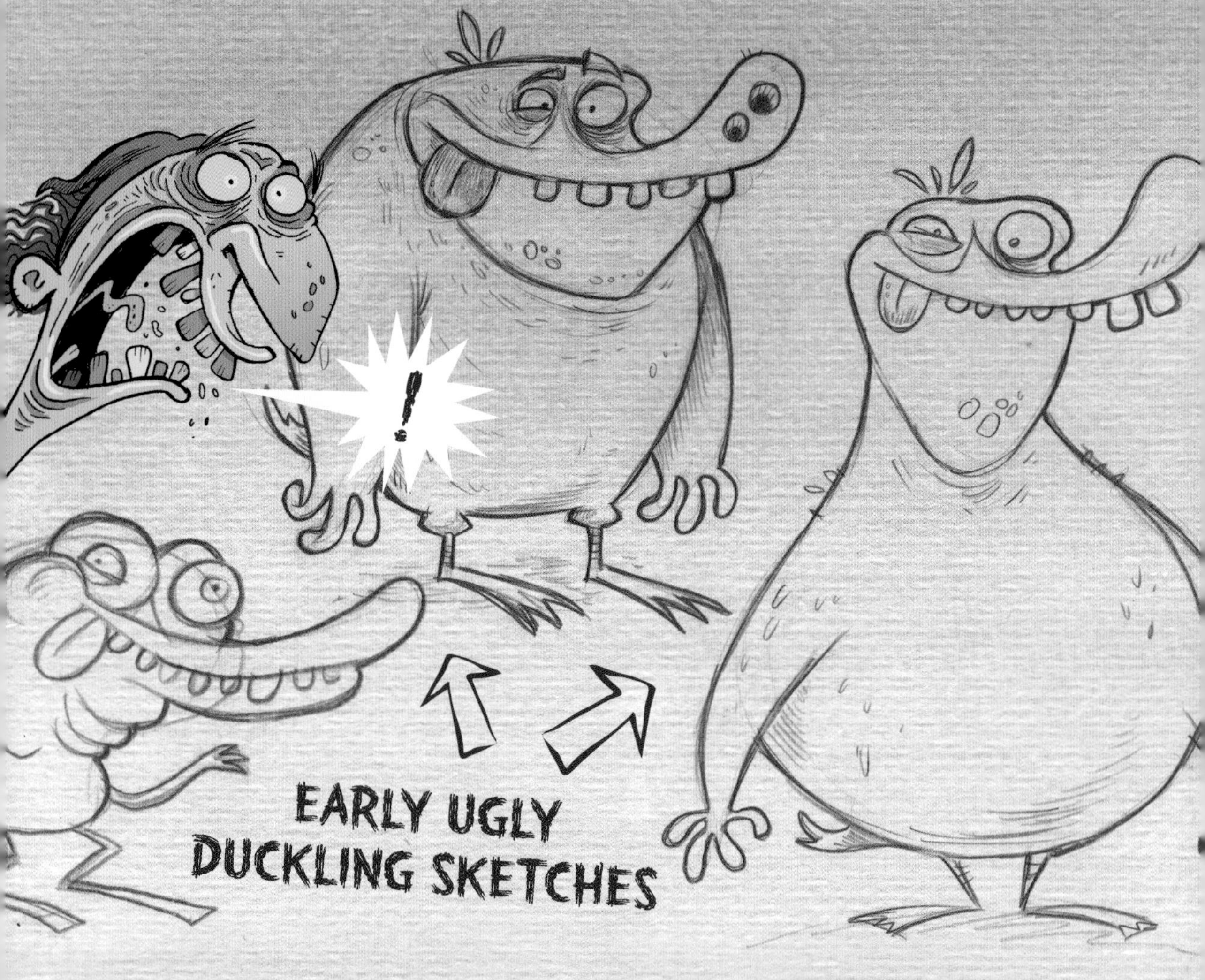
!

EARLY UGLY DUCKLING SKETCHES

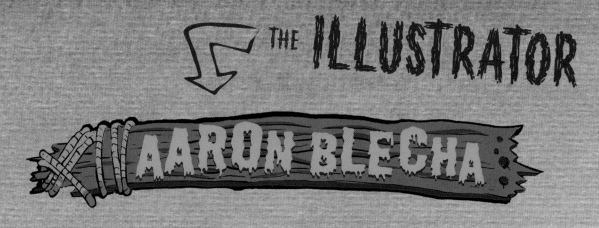

THE ILLUSTRATOR

AARON BLECHA

Aaron Blecha was raised by a school of slimy, yet gooey, giant squids in Wisconsin. Since then, Blecha has been working for more than ten years as an illustrator and designer for a hodgepodge of fun clients in the animation, publishing, toy, and entertainment industries. After many years in San Francisco, he now calls London his home.

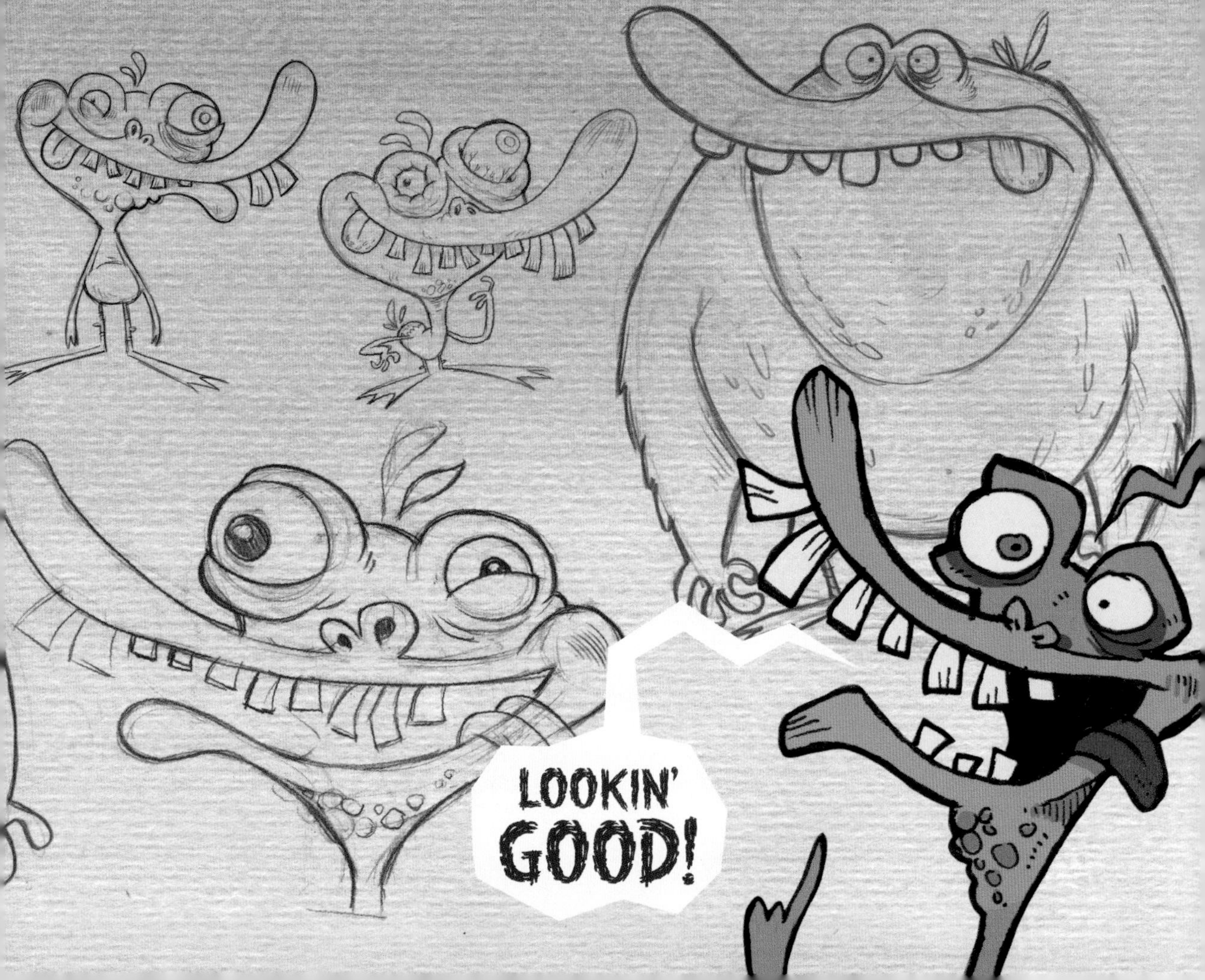
LOOKIN' GOOD!

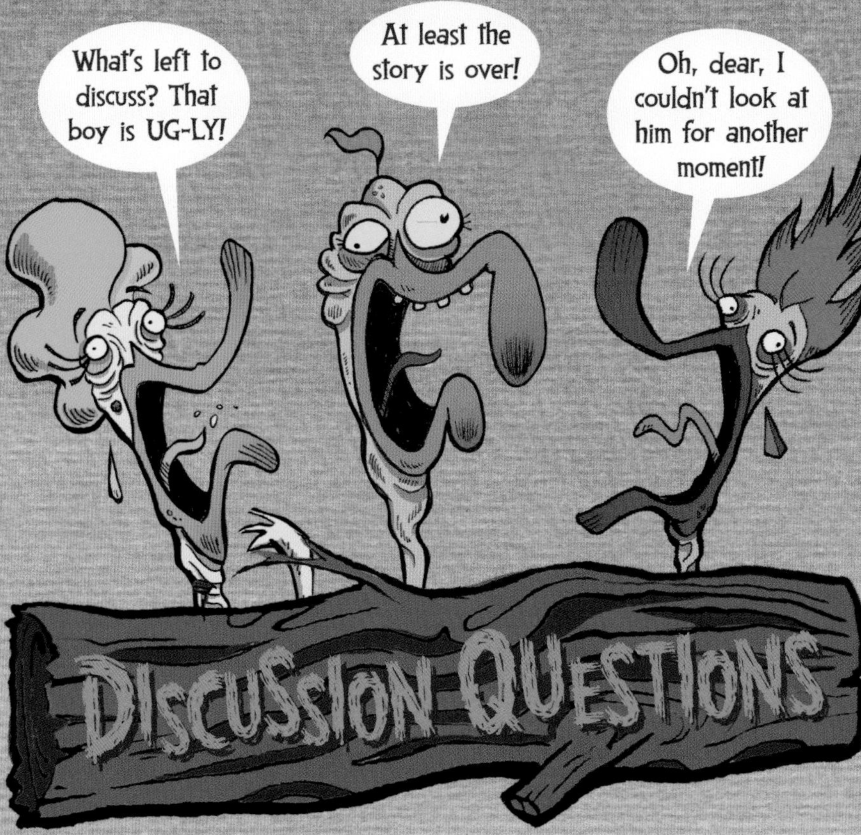
What's left to discuss? That boy is UG-LY!
At least the story is over!
Oh, dear, I couldn't look at him for another moment!
DISCUSSION QUESTIONS

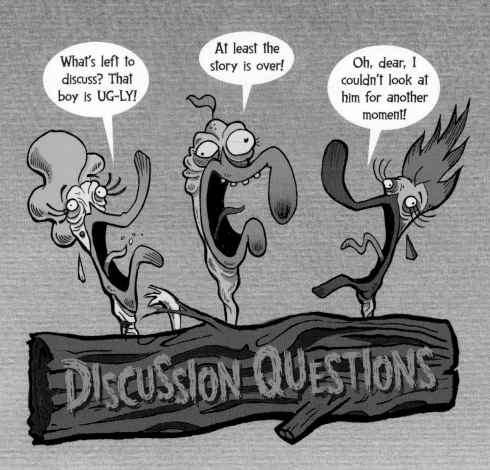

1. If you were the Ugly Duckling, would you have left the barnyard or stood up for yourself? Why do you think the Ugly Duckling decided to leave instead of facing his bullies?

2. Have you ever felt out of place like the Ugly Duckling? What did you do about it? How did you learn to fit in?

3. Each page of a graphic novel has several illustrations called panels. What was your favorite panel in this book? Describe the illustration and what you liked about it.

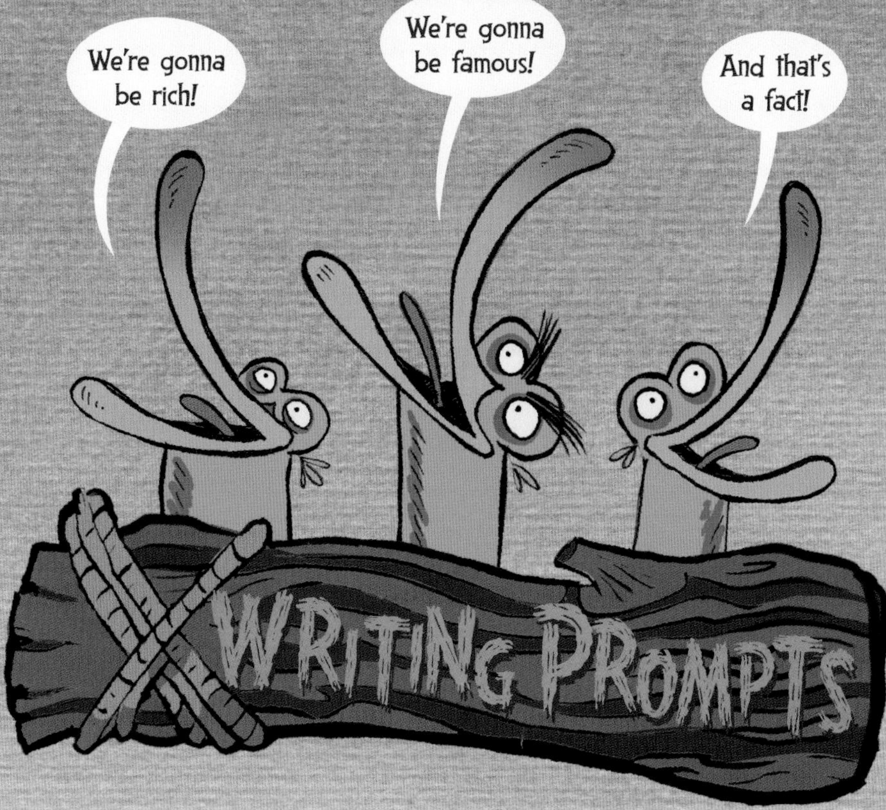
We're gonna be rich!
We're gonna be famous!
And that's a fact!
WRITING PROMPTS

1. Pretend you are the author and write a second part to this fairy tale. Does the Ugly Duckling live happily ever after? You decide.

2. Has anyone ever made fun of the way you look or act? Write about that moment and how it made you feel.

3. There are many different versions of the "Ugly Duckling" fairy tale. Write your own! What will your Ugly Duckling say or do? What will your Ugly Duckling look like? Use your imagination.

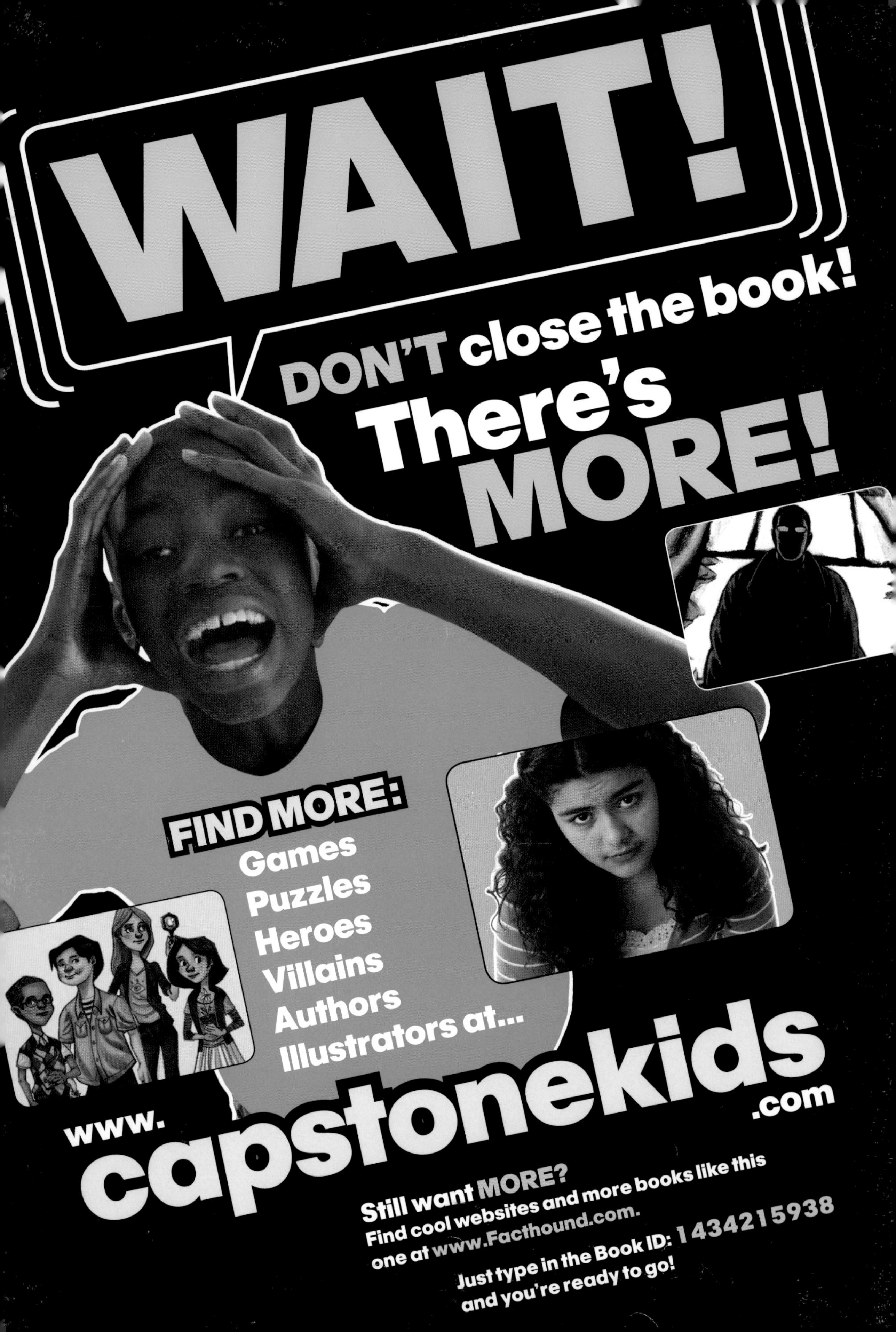
WAIT!
DON'T close the book!
There's MORE!
FIND MORE:
Games
Puzzles
Heroes
Villains
Authors
Illustrators at...
www.capstonekids.com
Still want MORE?
Find cool websites and more books like this one at www.Facthound.com.
Just type in the Book ID: 1434215938
and you're ready to go!